STOLEN BY THE ROGUE

A Regency Historical Romance

ROGUES OF THE ROAD

SASHA COTTMAN

Copyright © 2020 by Sasha Cottman

All rights reserved.

No part of this book may be reproduced in any form or by any electronic or mechanical means, including information storage and retrieval systems, without written permission from the author, except for the use of brief quotations in a book review.

To Dean and Laura

Prologue

London
September 1816

George Hawkins silently dropped from the top of the high brick wall and into the rear yard of the art gallery. His leather boots barely made a sound as they hit the ground. Crouching low, he glanced at the night sky and slyly grinned. The dark cover of a new moon was always welcome in his line of work. Tonight, was going to be good; he could feel it in his bones.

His enthusiasm ebbed just a touch as he caught a glimpse of light shining through the window of an upper floor. It was well past nine o'clock; the place should have been empty.

Come on. It's late. Don't you have a tasty supper waiting for you somewhere?

There was nothing worse than an over-efficacious security guard. Such men were the bane of George's career. How was a master thief supposed to get his hands on a lovely piece of lucre if some poorly paid night watchman was too keen to do his job properly?

He shifted to a spot against the wall where it was a little

darker and waited. Only a fool would risk taking a chance when an armed sentry was still on patrol. During one of his earlier reconnaissance missions, he had noticed that the guard in question had a pistol poking out from his jacket. Armed security at an art gallery—what was the world coming to?

"About bloody time," he muttered, when the light finally moved away.

He could just picture the man, lantern in hand, methodically checking every exhibition room as he made his way downstairs toward the front door and finally out into Oxford Street.

Good chap. Scuttle off home to your wife.

Not long now and George would have the place all to himself.

Reaching into his coat pocket, he fingered the set of skeleton keys he kept on his person at all times. His father had given them to George as a jest on the occasion of his sixteenth birthday. How a man who sat in judgement of thieves every day at the Old Bailey could find such a thing amusing, George had never been able to fathom. But he had politely accepted the keys and put them to good use almost straight away.

As he had done on many another night, George pushed the thought of his honest magistrate father to the back of his mind and refocused on the job at hand. Being the secret black sheep of the family came with its own price. He couldn't afford to suddenly grow a conscience when he was in the middle of a heist.

George gave it a respectable ten minutes before deciding it was safe to push off the wall and make his way to the back entrance. Still, he wasn't taking any chances, keeping to the shadowy edges of the yard and only coming out into the open when he was close to the rear entry.

A quick dash and he was standing at the door, keys at the ready.

And time for a professional pause.

He took a deep breath, then listened. Craftsmen always measured twice before cutting, while master thieves checked to make certain that they were not going to be disturbed.

Confident that he was indeed alone, George set a key to the lock. He smirked as the first one he chose fitted neatly into the hole and gave a satisfying click as it turned.

Every time, you pick it just right. George Hawkins, you are a clever lad.

Pushing the door open, he froze as the squeak of a tired hinge disturbed the perfect silence of the night. He gritted his teeth.

Bloody hell.

If he were the owner of this building, he would be having a firm word with the person tasked to oil the locks and latches. His heart thumped hard in his chest. At this stage of the operation, any sort of surprise wasn't a welcome one. He waited once more, carefully listening before stepping inside.

George closed the door behind him, wincing as it creaked again. He stilled, allowing his hearing to become accustomed to the little noises that the art gallery made. Buildings were living, breathing organisms with soft symphonies of their own. It took a special kind of mind to notice and understand them.

In order to become a successful criminal, a man had to develop both his hearing and his patience.

When he was certain that he was the only person in the building, George pressed ahead. One foot followed another as he made his way over to the wide oak staircase and began to ascend. Doing his best to ignore his racing heart, he slowly crept on.

Second door on the left. Far wall. Three frames over to the right. No need for a light.

He knew the painting well enough in the daylight, having visited the public showing on several occasions during the proceeding weeks. By attending during the busiest periods, he had been able to conceal himself within the crowded ranks of gallery visitors. It had also given George the chance to watch the guards while remaining out of sight of their prying eyes.

After entering the exhibition space, he crossed the floor then came to a halt in front of the third mounted painting. He stared at it for a time, then softly sighed.

Titian's *Venus with a Mirror* never failed to make him happy.

It was a masterful representation of the goddess, naked while studying herself in a mirror. Titian had reached the pinnacle of his career with the use of rich colors and subject. When he caught a glimpse of Venus's breasts in the dull light, George licked his lips.

Now there was a man who appreciated the naked female form.

And if the masterful work of the artist's brush wasn't enough, the fact that the painting was worth a small fortune was enough of a reason to make a professional thief smile. If George could steal it, and find a willing buyer, all his money problems would be over.

He leaned in close.

Forty-nine inches by forty-one. The perfect size for a one-man mission.

With one hand resting on the top of the frame, the other supporting its weight, he lifted the painting up and away from its mount before setting it gently onto the floor.

BANG!

He whirled round. Someone had slammed the front door. Heavy footsteps echoed on the stairs.

"Bloody ridiculous. Fancy forgetting your dinner tin. She'll have my guts for garters if I come home without it," a low voice chastised.

"Bugger," George muttered.

The potbellied guard had returned. If George remained

where he was, the man would pass by the door on the way to the storeroom. He would surely see a night thief, priceless painting at his feet, and all hell would break loose.

Quickly abandoning the Titian, George made for the opposite wall, praying that if the guard did happen to step into the room, he may by some miracle be able to slip out behind the man and leave unnoticed.

The footsteps came closer. George's heart beat hard and fast in his chest. All his worst nightmares were fast becoming reality. A large bead of sweat trickled down his spine.

Back pressed hard against the wall, he inched his way closer to the door, ready to bolt the second the watchman entered the room.

The footsteps stopped a mere yard or so away out in the hall.

"What the devil is going on?" said the man.

Bloody. Bloody. Bollocks.

George waited until his adversary had made it all the way into the room and was standing, hands on rounded hips, looking down at the painting before finally making his move. He took three deft steps to his left and bolted for the door.

"Hey! Stop, thief!"

He leapt down the staircase, dropping with a hard thud onto the first main landing before scurrying for the next set of risers. Footsteps thudded close behind.

A bullet pinged over his head and into the mahogany wood of the wall ahead of him. George didn't stop to count his blessings. Instead, he focused his gaze and prayers solely on the front door.

"Sweet Lord let it be unlocked," he muttered.

If the guard had secured the door behind him when he returned, George was going to be in serious trouble. Fighting his way out of the gallery would be his only option. The sound of the man's footsteps grew louder as he closed the distance between them.

"Come back here, you villain. I'll skin you alive!"

The angry guard was close on his heels when George reached for the handle. He almost wept for joy when it turned, and the door swung open. A gust of cold night air smacked him in the face, but he paid it no mind. Only escape mattered.

He raced out into the street, ignoring the foul curses and loud shouts coming from behind him. No, he wasn't going to stop or come back, thank you very much. With legs pumping and arms swinging, he ran at full stretch along Oxford Street, darting out into the road when other late-night strollers impeded his progress.

At Argyle Street, he made a sharp right turn. The path ahead was clear of pedestrians. Digging deep into what was left of his energy reserves, George increased his pace.

He ran straight past the front door of his home and continued on at breakneck speed, only slowing to take the corner into Great Marlborough Street. After ducking out of sight into the doorway of a shop, he finally came to a skittering halt.

As he bent, hands on knees, and tried to catch his breath, he kept his gaze fixed firmly on the street. To his bone-deep relief, there was no sign of his pursuer.

George panted and wheezed as he sucked in one great lungful of air after the other. The adrenaline coursing through his body made him nauseous. If he hadn't been in the middle of a London street, he would have given in to temptation and cast up his accounts.

Several minutes passed before his heart rate finally returned to normal. His days of being a champion athlete at school and the resultant muscle memory had saved him tonight, but it had been a near-run thing. His fitness wasn't anywhere near as good as it had once been.

Thank God that guard couldn't fire a pistol to save himself, let alone stop an art thief.

In all his years of thieving and smuggling, he had never come this close to being caught. Or shot.

I must have missed something or not waited long enough. Heavens, am I losing my touch?

After a quick wipe of his face with a handkerchief, George straightened his attire and made ready to go home. There was little point in wasting any more time standing out in the street. All his careful planning and preparation had come to naught. The Titian would never be his.

You escaped with your life. Be grateful for that large blessing.

He checked at the corner of Argyle Street and found it was clear. The overweight and unfit guard hadn't been able to keep up with him.

That was too bloody close for anyone's liking. What if he had been a better shot? I might well be dead.

He took in a deep, calming breath and straightened his shoulders.

By the time George Hawkins reached his home at number 45 Argyle Street, his pace had dropped to that of a leisurely saunter.

Only a fool would come tearing in the front door of his father's house as if the hounds of hell were hot on his tail.

He nodded at the footman who answered the door, giving him a friendly grin as he stepped inside. But George's self-assured smile froze on his lips when his gaze settled on the crowd of people who were gathered in the foyer and main ballroom of the Hawkins family home.

Everywhere he looked there was a senior member of the London judiciary. Magistrates, barristers, and even a smattering of King's Counsels stood shoulder to shoulder, drinking and laughing.

Hell, and the devil. I forgot the legal soiree was on tonight.

The sick, heavy feeling in the pit of his stomach returned. If things had not gone his way just a few minutes earlier, he may well have found himself being hauled up in front of one of his father's friends and made to face judgement.

And I would have been found guilty.

His mother appeared from out of the crowd. She took one look at him, frowned, and hurried to his side. "George, my sweet boy, you don't look at all well. Are you coming down with something?"

"No, I just . . ."

Before he could stop her, Mrs. Hawkins had placed a hand on George's brow. She shook her head and tutted. "Definitely warm and a little sweaty. Maybe you should head upstairs to bed. An early night might be in order. Just remember I am having Lady Dodd and her daughter, Petunia, over tomorrow afternoon, and you did promise to stop by and give them your regards."

Not another matchmaking attempt, Mama. Please. I don't need you to find me a wife.

"Perhaps I should make it an early night. Though if I am still not right in the morning, you may have to give Lady Dodd my sincere apologies," he replied.

Anything he did to avoid having to take tea and cake with yet another young miss on his mother's ever-growing list of potential brides was worth it. A good son shouldn't lie to his mother about being ill, but George had told so many untruths to his parents over the years that they rolled off his tongue without a second thought.

I really am the worst of the family.

He was about to make good on his promise to head upstairs when the Honorable Judge Hawkins hailed him from the doorway of the ballroom. "Ah! George, I was wondering if you were going to make it home in time for my little gathering. Good to see you, son." He hurried over.

Mrs. Hawkins turned to her husband. "I think George is unwell. I suggested he should turn in."

The look of disappointment on his father's face put a swift

end to George's plans for a speedy exit. He hadn't done the expected thing and followed his father and brother into the legal fraternity. And while Judge Hawkins made obvious attempts to hide his feelings, it was clear to George that his sire still hadn't come to terms with his youngest son's rejection of the family calling.

"I am certain I could manage one drink," replied George.

His father's demeanor changed in an instant. "Excellent. Grab a glass and come and say a quick hello to the Lord High Chancellor. Lord Eldon was just about to tell us the story of a wicked jewel thief they executed at Newgate Prison this morning. I am sure you will find it fascinating."

If caught, I would have been sentenced. And I would have been hung.

A reluctant George took a brandy from a footman and followed his father into the ballroom. He could just imagine how it would feel to be a condemned man taking his final steps on the way to the scaffold.

That could've been me.

"Lord Eldon, you remember my son George, don't you?" said his father.

George stirred from his horrid imaginings of death and bowed low. "My lord."

As he righted himself, his gaze met that of the man who, aside from the King, was the most powerful legal authority in all of England—a man who one day could very well hold George's fate in his hands. It wouldn't matter if he was the son of a judge; he would not be shown any mercy.

He swallowed deeply as grey, all-seeing eyes stared back at him. And in that moment, George Hawkins made a fateful decision.

I have to find another way to make money or I am destined to end up swinging by my neck at the end of a rope. I must give up this life of villainy. But how?

Chapter One

A week later
The RR Coaching Company Offices
Gracechurch Street, London

"Just be grateful you are here and not in Newgate Prison," said Harry.

George lifted his head from where it had been sitting in his hands and glared at his fellow rogue of the road. Lord Harry Steele, son of the Duke of Redditch, was the only member of the RR Coaching Company currently making any real effort at earning an honest living. His words, though clearly meant to be kind, were not the least bit welcome.

"Yes, well, it's alright for you; your wife is an heiress. Her papa is one of the richest men in all of England. You will never have to worry about money," replied George.

Not to mention that I am the one with an outstanding obligation to buy the next travel coach for the company. I have no idea where I am going to find the money.

With a sigh, Harry dropped into the seat next to George at

the long, weather-beaten dining table that took up most of the space in the main room of the company offices.

"Let me assure you that Mister North is not that free with his blunt. In fact, he keeps Alice and I on a tight leash when it comes to money."

Harry had married one of his clients earlier in the year; and while Alice was a wonderful girl, she had come with an ironclad marriage contract that didn't include a large dowry settlement. Mister North had made certain that his daughters would not fall to the charms of fortune hunters and make poor choices when it came to husbands.

"As long as you stay in Daddy North's good graces, the money will keep coming," replied George.

He wasn't in the mood for any attempt at being upbeat. The near miss at the art gallery had rocked his self-confidence more than he wished to admit.

And to top the evening off, instead of managing to slink upstairs, George's guilt had seen him remain for several hours at his father's party while every senior London judge enquired as to why he had not taken up the legal profession. Unfortunately, it was a question to which George couldn't give a truthful answer.

Because I would rather steal bright and shiny things than waste my existence on reading boring legal papers.

His life was all too complicated.

Unless he could find himself a nice, rich girl to marry, he was going to be forced to continue doing dirty jobs for the RR Coaching Company and run the risk of one day getting caught. The other option, of course, being to secure himself an honest job.

Until now, that option had held little appeal; but a close call with a bullet could give a man cause to rethink many things in his life.

Could I live an honest life?

He was the son of a judge, and yet he had always been

tempted by the illegal and illicit side of life. The rush of handling stolen goods gave him a high that only the heated embrace of a woman could challenge or surpass. And since valuable trinkets were much easier to manage than women, George had made a lifelong habit of avoiding emotional entanglements with the fairer sex.

But if you don't change, you are going to meet a sticky end.

"I just need to find a way to make enough money so I can turn my life around," he muttered.

"What did you say?" replied Harry.

"Nothing."

The door of the office opened and through it stepped Andrew McNeal, the Duke of Monsale. He was followed by the bulking form of Sir Stephen Moore carrying a newspaper. Trailing behind Stephen was a young boy. George noted the look of displeasure written across the child's face. In his hand was a small chalkboard on which several unsuccessful attempts at the letter 'B' had been made.

"Now, Toby, I know you don't want to sit and practice your letters, but as a gentleman, you must learn to read and write," said Stephen. He held the newspaper aloft. "Because when you can read, you will be able to sit at the breakfast table and scour the daily newspaper from cover to cover. That is what all men of quality do first thing each morning."

Stephen grandly tossed the paper onto the table where it landed with a crisp *thwack* close to where George sat.

George did his best to stifle a laugh. Hearing one of London's foremost rakes trying to teach his newly acquired ward about being a gentleman had become the source of much amusement amongst the rogues of the road over the past few weeks.

Monsale passed by the table, a sly grin on his face. He gave George a wink as he continued on toward the kitchen. Monsale was not one for exchanging words until he had downed his first coffee of the day.

"But Sir Stephen, can't I just go and help Bob muck out the stables?" pleaded Toby.

Harry rose from the table and held out his arms. "I thought you were coming home with me today. Lady Alice will be waiting. She so looks forward to your visits. Besides, cook made a fruit bun especially for you this morning, and you wouldn't want to disappoint her, now, would you?"

The petulant look on Toby's face immediately dissipated, replaced by wide-eyed excitement. "I'll get my coat," he cried. The chalkboard was discarded on the table without a second look as he dashed out of the room and down the hall.

A chuckling Monsale reappeared from the kitchen carrying a mug of steaming coffee in his hand. "The way to a boy's heart is through his stomach."

Yes, but that boy stole your affection the moment you met him.

Monsale might have been all puff and bluster, but George suspected that beneath his gruff exterior lived a warm heart. One which he, at times, struggled to hide. It was comforting to know that the trauma of Monsale's violent upbringing had not completely turned him to stone.

Someday, my friend, you might even be brave enough to risk giving your heart to a woman.

Stephen picked up the chalkboard and, after giving Toby's handwriting a disapproving scowl, wiped it clean with the palm of his hand. "Well, if the boy will sit and pay attention to his lessons, I would be more than happy to give him a whole sticky bun for breakfast every morning."

If only all of life's troubles could be solved with a piece of warm fruit bun and some tasty cheese.

Monsale set his coffee cup down across from George's place at the table before taking a seat. George ran his finger over the nearest knife mark on the table, staring intently at it as he avoided meeting Monsale's enquiring gaze. He didn't need to look up to know his friend's eyes were boring into him.

The duke sighed. "Don't tell me you are still sulking over that mishap last week?"

Harry reached over and gave George a friendly pat on the shoulder. "You outran the chap and got away. I don't see why you are still in the dumps. It's almost as if you are disappointed that you didn't get caught."

George lifted his gaze. There was no point trying to ignore his friends.

The fair-haired Monsale sat back in his chair, wagging a finger in George's direction. "You are badly in need of a Hannibal moment in your life."

A Hannibal what?

He waited while Monsale took a long sip of his brew before asking the obvious. "I know I am going to regret asking this, but what on earth is a Hannibal moment?"

Monsale chuckled. "Well, Hannibal of Carthage needed to find a way to invade Italy. The easiest way would have been to sail across the Mediterranean and land in Sicily, but then he would have been met by a huge Roman force. Instead, he came over the Alps."

"But he didn't succeed in sacking Rome. I'm not sure if he is the right example to be using if what you are aiming for is a lesson in turning failure into fortune," said Harry.

George nodded. "Not to mention the fact that while he did it in style with thousands of soldiers and thirty-eight elephants, half his army and most of the poor beasts didn't make it into Italy. But, yes, I get the gist of what you are saying. I need to approach my problem from a different angle," said George.

Monsale nodded. "Exactly. I think . . ."

The room fell silent as Toby reappeared. The members of the RR Coaching Company had all agreed not to discuss their illegal business dealings in front of the boy. Young minds were too impressionable.

Stephen bent to help Toby with his coat buttons. "Where is your scarf?" he said.

Toby frowned. "I don't know."

Harry dug a hand into his pocket and produced a navy-blue woolen scarf. "You left it at our house yesterday."

He handed it to Stephen, who quickly wrapped it around Toby's neck. He patted his young ward gently on the head. "Now, are you ready to take your leave properly?" Stephen stepped back, and an expectant hush fell over the room.

Toby straightened his posture and then bowed firstly to Stephen and then the others. "Thank you, gentlemen. I bid you a good day."

Harry took Toby by the hand and led him to the door. He turned and nodded at Stephen. "Send word if your plans change and you cannot collect Toby before supper tomorrow; Alice and I are more than happy for him to stay a second night."

"Will do and give my best regards to your ever-patient wife."

George kept his gaze on the door long after Harry and Toby had left. He was badly in need of a distraction. With the small boy gone, it wouldn't be long before Monsale decided to wade back into George's misery and offer him yet more of his unsolicited advice.

"As I was saying. You need something to get you out of this rut. Your life lacks purpose. And you owe the RR Coaching Company a new coach, which at the moment doesn't appear to be arriving any time soon," said Monsale.

The head of the rogues of the road was never going to let George forget his contractual obligations. Every member of the company had to provide a coach as part of their buy-in money.

Can't you just leave me to wallow in my despair for five minutes? If it's not too much of an indulgence.

But as much as it pained him to admit it, Monsale was right. He was in a rut.

His career as a master thief had once been full of vigor, but with the war in Europe now over, his steady supply of stolen items from France and Spain had all but dried up, and with them so had his passion.

People no longer had the pressing need to engage his services to steal or smuggle precious goods out of the continent. Over the past year, business had gone from bad to terrible.

It left him aimless, and if he was honest about it, more than a little scared.

"I hear you, Monsale. I just don't know what I can do about it. Apart from almost getting caught the other night, I am also facing a serious cashflow problem. Meaning, I basically have none. All my recent jobs have either paid poorly or not at all. And the only other available avenues, such as stealing to order, are becoming far too dangerous," he replied.

The truth was that for all his illicit behavior, George considered anything that was not of his own volition to be, well, beneath him. Oddly, for a career criminal, George prided himself on the quality of his work, on the creativity behind it. He would never stoop to the dull and less financially lucrative level of picking pockets or robbing people's houses.

The art gallery job had been a first for George. He admired the artist Titian and had planned to hold onto the painting for a short time before eventually selling it to someone who could give him a good price.

There was a lucrative market for stolen artwork both in England and overseas. Buyers with deep pockets would have been lining up to buy *Venus with a Mirror*.

'Twas not to be.

His fingers carelessly settled on the top of the newspaper, and he glanced over at it. A headline partway down the second column on the front page caught his attention.

. . .

A SPECIAL OTTOMAN EXHIBITION
From the private collection of the Sultan, Mahmud II,
Treasures of the East. An exhibition of antiquities, including the
priceless gold and jewel-encrusted crown of Baldwin I (crusader
ruler of Constantinople).
At the Ottoman Embassy, Adelphi Buildings, nr. the Strand.
J. Scott. Esq. Curator and Antiquities expert.

What if I could get my hands on some ancient treasure? Surely something like that would be worth pinching, and there must be a market for it.

"Now that would solve all of my problems," he muttered.

He cleared his throat. "Monsale, do you still have that connection who deals in finding new homes for dusty old artifacts?"

"Yes, why?"

"No reason. Just asking." He rose from the table, suddenly in need of a second strong cup of tea.

Escaping from home early most mornings in order to avoid his father meant George usually purchased a hot bun for breakfast on the way over to the RR Coaching Company offices. This morning, however, he had been in such a low mood that even food couldn't spark his interest. Now he was hungry.

Hungry for change.

He filled his cup quickly before returning to stand next to the table where he picked up the newspaper once more. He met Stephen's gaze. "You don't mind if I keep this, do you? I agree with what you told Toby. A gentleman should peruse the paper properly each day."

Stephen raised an eyebrow and gave him a wary look.

"Just because you are the Honorable George Hawkins doesn't make you a gentleman, but yes keep *The Times*. Are you going to look in the *Want Places* section for a respectable role?"

George ignored the smart quip and tucked the paper firmly under his arm. He had no time left for sitting idly and chatting. "You never know what you might find in the newspaper."

And with that he downed a mouthful of the tea, set his cup on the table, and headed for the door. He had a plan, and that plan involved finding out all he could about the Ottoman Empire before making the acquaintance of Mister J. Scott, antiquities expert.

And then I intend to get my hands on that golden crown.

Chapter Two

J ane read the advertisement in *The Times* once more and grinned. In a matter of days, she would be overseeing her first real exhibition of archeological artifacts. And it was in London.

Excitement bubbled in her stomach.

J. Scott. Esq. Curator and Antiquities expert.

The words were only a partial lie. She wasn't an esquire, but she certainly knew more about the Ottoman treasures than any of the scholars attached to the British Museum. They had turned their noses up when she'd offered to present an exhibition of articles from Constantinople and Lebanon. She was still fuming over the condescending way in which they had dealt with her. One had even laughed as she picked up her papers and, red-faced, hurried from the offices of the museum.

"*Günaydın*, Miss Scott."

She turned as the Ottoman ambassador stepped into the room. "Good morning, your excellency."

He pointed at the newspaper. "I see our little notice made the front page. Hopefully we will get some people to come and visit the exhibition. Pottery and stone tablets aren't particularly exciting, but who knows? We might manage to get a spot of interest in the crown."

Jane's gaze shifted to the large glass box that sat in the center of the room, and she softly smiled. Resting on a piece of red silk cloth sat the jewel of the exhibition, her pride and joy. "If the crowds at the Tower of London queuing to see the crown jewels are anything to go by, we know that the English love their royal splendor. Rest assured, your excellency—they will want to see Baldwin's crown."

I hope they do. Otherwise, the exhibition will be a failure, as will I.

If the various pieces of ancient pottery in the other display cases had been all she had to offer, the ambassador would likely have been right in having reservations. The crusader, Baldwin, had been invested as ruler of Constantinople early in the thirteenth century. His gold crown was a major drawcard.

It had cost an extra shilling to put the notice on the front page of *The Times*; a calculated risk, which Jane was confident would pay off. The sultan wanted people in London to not only see items of cultural importance, but to know that he was a wealthy and powerful ruler. The crown was a clear statement of the magnificence of the Ottoman empire, something designed to impress.

Hopefully it will also gain me a better-paying position in London society once this exhibition is over.

England was a hard place for a young woman without proper connections or money to survive. The Sultan's offer for her to help curate this display could not have come at a better time for Jane. She had been between paid employment and down to a few pennies when the opportunity had presented itself. Her last role as governess to a pair of overindulged and spoilt eleven-year-old girls had been enough for her to decide she had to find another way to make a living.

If only the British Museum would take on a female scholar.

She had prayed for that miracle more times than she cared to count, but every application she submitted always came back as a polite refusal. Women had no place in archeology.

Unless something new dropped into her lap, she was destined to end up working in a bookshop or as an unofficial, underpaid guide showing guests around the museum.

"Well, I had better get on with completing the rest of the information cards today, your excellency. People might find the pottery pieces a bit more interesting if they knew where they had come from and how people living in Byblos actually used them," she said.

With the exhibition due to open in two days, her focus had to be on doing everything to ensure it was a popular sensation, one which would draw large crowds. If the first visitors could be suitably impressed, then word of mouth might serve to attract more patrons.

If I can make this a success, I might be able to get myself established back in England and finally meet the right people. People who can help with my quest.

The quest had begun with her late father, and Jane had vowed to complete it.

The rumors were true. The secret letter was real. She had even managed to find the cypher with which to unlock the letter's coded message.

Jane had painstakingly put together all the clues and was anxious to move forward with the search. The only thing she lacked—money.

If she could just find one person with cash to spare whom she could trust, there would be nothing left between her and claiming a king's long-lost treasure.

Chapter Three

George shivered as the breeze from the River Thames whipped through his shirt. It had been a particularly warm September day, and he had foolishly not thought to wear a coat this evening. He did his best to ignore Harry's disapproving snort as he stepped down from the carriage. At least Harry's wife, Alice, was kind enough to gift him a sympathetic smile as George hurriedly buttoned his jacket.

I hope it's warm inside the embassy. Otherwise, it's going to be a long, cold night.

The striking, three-storied Adelphi buildings complex in which the Ottoman embassy was housed towered over them. The block of eleven unified houses fronted a vaulted terrace along the riverbank, under which a series of wharves had been built. Situated between the Strand and the River Thames, the Adelphi could be seen from miles downriver. It was an imposing sight.

"Do you have the tickets?" asked Harry.

Alice nodded and, after reaching into her reticule, handed one to both her husband and George.

The exhibition had only been going for four days, but it had quickly become one of the hottest attractions in town.

Having been unsuccessful in managing to secure a ticket for himself, George had been most relieved when Alice's sister Patience had cried off this evening and the spare ticket had been offered to him.

He followed Alice and Harry up the front steps of the Ottoman embassy and through the front door. They stood patiently at the end of a short line, waiting to be admitted to the exhibition space.

It was just after seven o'clock, and George was pleased that the gathering inside the embassy wasn't too large. He caught Harry's eye.

"We must be getting old. When did we start attending any social event this side of ten o'clock in the evening?" he said.

Harry raised an eyebrow, then glanced at his wife and the swell of her belly. Alice was heavily pregnant with their first child, and the couple rarely stayed out late these days. Lord Harry Steele now arrived early each morning at the offices of the RR Coaching Company and was usually the first one to leave midafternoon.

His fellow rogue of the road had all but given up on any of the company's illicit work the moment he'd married Alice. Harry's new role consisted of managing the growing coaching side of the business and seeking honest investments to add to their cash reserves. Things had certainly changed for the former scandal-maker.

Alice yawned. "I am terrible. The number of times I have fallen asleep just after supper is ridiculous. And to think I used to be able to stay out all night and welcome the dawn."

Harry bent and placed a tender kiss on his wife's cheek, causing George to avert his gaze.

"You are glowing with the promise of life. That takes a lot of energy, my love," Harry said.

A tinge of unexpected jealousy pricked at George. He couldn't begrudge his friend's happiness, but it brought his own empty existence into sharp relief. He was thankful when they were called to the front of the line and asked for their tickets.

The Ottoman Royal Exhibition, as had been printed on the tickets, was on display in three separate rooms. Inside the first of these was a selection of carefully curated pieces of pottery, stone tablets, and a handful of paintings.

While Harry and Alice walked arm in arm around the room, George took the opportunity to spend some time on his own. From his jacket pocket, he produced a pencil and a notebook. If anyone chanced a look in his direction, they might think him perhaps an amateur scholar bent over the display case while busily taking notes.

What he was actually doing was making rough sketches of the room and noting where things were placed. His scribblings included the number of guards, of which there were only two, as well as the location of doors and windows.

After his close run with the art gallery guard, George had decided that he needed to have several escape routes mapped out when he attempted to rob the embassy.

"I see you find the spice bowls of interest," said a female voice.

He hastily tucked the notebook into his jacket pocket before righting himself and turning.

A vision of stunning beauty swept his breath away. For a moment he just stood staring, speechless. Talk about being struck by lightning.

"Are you alright, sir?" she asked.

How am I to reply when my mind and mouth have stopped working together?

George blinked out of his stupor. "Yes, I am fine. I just . . ." His brain was too busy processing the sheer loveliness of the woman who stood in front of him. A thousand words to describe her long brown tresses whirled about in his mind.

And when it came to the sprinkle of delightful freckles that kissed either side of her nose, the right word eluded him.

Caramel. Chocolate. Coffee.

"Did you want to know more about the spice bowls?" she asked.

"Cinnamon?" he ventured.

Her brows furrowed, then she softly chortled. "Sometimes, though cinnamon did actually originate in the Far East. It is native to Ceylon and some parts of India. These bowls would have been used to hold spices such as cumin, cardamon, and, of course, black pepper. Many of these spices still form the basis of Ottoman dishes today."

George could cheerfully stand here all night and listen to this woman babble on about herbs and spices. She was utterly captivating.

He took a hurried step back when Harry and Alice suddenly appeared from the midst of the crowd. Alice held out her hand. "Hello, I am Lady Alice Steele, and this is my husband, Harry. It is a pleasure to hear a female speak with such authority on a subject. You seem to know an awful lot about the exhibition."

The woman dipped into a deep curtesy at the mention of Alice's title.

"Jane Scott, Lady Alice. I am the curator of his majesty's collection," she replied.

"You are J. Scott? When I read the advertisement, I assumed you were a man," said George.

Jane screwed up her face. "Yes. I wasn't sure that would come to see the items if I put my real name in the newspaper. Fortunately, it doesn't appear to have stopped people from recommending the show once they have been here."

"That was rather clever of you," replied Harry.

She blinked slowly as her gaze took in the bright green floral shirt which Lord Harry Steele wore under his jacket. Marriage might have tamed some of Harry's eccentric behavior, but he was still one for dressing outrageously. George was grateful that his friend had at least decided to leave the matching silk top hat at home.

"I have discovered that many London folk only take you at first blush. If they thought a woman was curating this important work, they might give it a miss. I apologize for the slight deception," said Jane.

George and Harry exchanged a knowing look. Neither was going to condemn someone for practicing the very thing which they had built their careers upon.

When her gaze turned back to him, George felt an uncommon sense of discomfort. He wasn't used to being awkward around women. But this Jane Scott was a female of a variety entirely new to his experience. A woman of beauty, intelligence, and something else.

"And you are?" she asked.

A dolt who cannot remember his manners when it comes to meeting women and actually making formal introductions.

He bowed his head. "The Honorable George Hawkins at your service, Miss Scott."

Her pale grey-green eyes flashed with an unmistakable hint of interest. For all the times that he'd privately hated coming from a family of judges, right now George was more than happy to add the honorable moniker to his name. Anything to get Jane Scott's attention and hold it.

Now if he could just get Alice and Harry to go away—he might stand a chance at chatting her up.

How can I get rid of them without causing offence?

Alice and her baby belly moved closer. "Tell me, Jane, how is it that you have come to be in London and working for the supreme ruler of the Ottoman Empire? I note a hint of a foreign accent in your speech."

Jane nodded. "I was born here in London but spent most of my life living in Byblos in the Eyalet of Sidon. It is on the Mediterranean Sea, about fifty miles north west of Damascus.

My father was an antiquities advisor to the sultan. The pieces of pottery are from the dig at Byblos castle."

From the obvious *was* in her last sentence, and the touch of sadness in Jane's voice at the mention of her father, George would bet a penny that Mister Scott was no longer amongst the living.

And odd that she didn't say anything about the rest of her family.

Who are you? I want to know more about you.

Jane gave a shy, awkward smile. "But enough about me; I am sure you are not here to listen to my ramblings. Would you like to see Baldwin's magnificent gold and jeweled-encrusted crown?"

"Yes please," replied Alice.

George followed Harry and Alice as Jane led them into a second room. For someone who had arrived only a short while ago, firmly intent on an evening of sly reconnaissance, he suddenly found himself unable to keep his focus solely on the idea of stealing the crown. His attention was stuck on the delightful form of Miss Jane Scott.

Now there is a prize worth capturing.

Chapter Four

Jane stepped into the second display room and held out her hand.

"My lord, lady, and honorable gentleman, may I present to you the crown of Baldwin the First," she announced proudly.

She loved this moment. Witnessing people's reactions to their first sight of the precious jewel always gave her a secret thrill.

Lord Harry and Lady Alice exchanged excited grins then rushed into the space and right up against the red rope, which kept visitors at a respectable distance from the crown. Wide-eyed, they craned their necks and gazed at Baldwin's prize. Jane came and stood next to them. George walked into the room but oddly took up a spot at the rear.

"Fantastic," said Harry.

"I'm so glad we came," replied his wife.

The decision to put the crown out of reach of visitors had not been an easy one, but a nervous Ottoman ambassador had firmly insisted upon it. If someone was to damage the crown or heaven forbid attempt to steal it, he would be the one to suffer the wrath of the sultan.

Thank goodness he finally relented and let me display it on a raised dais rather than have it in a glass case.

On the wall behind the exhibit hung a large red and white flag bearing the Imperial Standard. That had been Jane's suggestion—an imposing display of the wealth and power of the Ottoman Empire.

Lord Harry clapped his hands together. "Oh gosh, that's splendid! How old did you say it was?"

Jane moved to one side, creating a space for the third member of the party, but George Hawkins remained where he was at the back of the room. He didn't seem half as impressed about the exhibition as his friends.

"Baldwin was crowned at Hagia Sophia in twelve-O-four, so it is well over six hundred years old." She motioned to the space she had just vacated. "Please, Mister Hawkins, feel free to come and stand here. You should be able to see things quite well from this vantage point."

He shook his head as if coming out of a daze before moving forward.

Perhaps he had a few too many wines at supper. He certainly doesn't seem that interested in the crown. How strange.

"What are the jewels in the piece?" asked Lady Alice.

Jane opened her mouth, ready to give the standard reply.

"Rubies, and various colored sapphires by the look of it," said George.

So, you have been paying attention. And you know your jewels.

"Um, yes. And there was a ring of emeralds around the base at one point, but most of them disappeared over the years. In the fifteenth century, the ruling sultan had the rest taken out to make the crown look neater," added Jane. How anyone could consider making alterations to such an important historical artifact was beyond her. It was cultural vandalism in the name of making something look pretty. "Are you a collector of precious stones, Mister Hawkins? You seem to have an eye for them."

Lord Harry coughed loudly into his elbow, and Jane caught the hard glare his wife gave him. *What a curious group of people.*

"I am afraid my pocket doesn't permit me to collect much more than the odd ball of lint at the moment, let alone a ruby or two," replied George.

Jane quietly studied him for a moment, taking the peculiarly behaved visitor in. He was tall in comparison to most other men, likely a good six foot two. His broad shoulders were displayed to perfection by his tailored jacket, which she was privately pleased he had unbuttoned since his arrival.

Her gaze drifted to the top of his trousers, lingering appreciatively for a few seconds before shifting upwards. Short brown hair, a shade or two darker than her own, was matched by his deep hazel eyes, which stared back at her.

Oh.

"How could one put a price on such a treasured item if you were ever inclined to sell it? It must be worth a fortune," he added.

"The sultan would never willingly part with it, so I guess we shall never know," she replied.

You are a handsome devil, even if you do make me feel uncomfortable.

Jane gathered her thoughts and wits. "Now, I can allow you a few minutes more in here, but the next group of ticket holders will be coming along shortly. Of course, if you wish to visit again, we will have more showings later in the week before we close the exhibition."

A frown appeared on George's face. "When does the exhibition end?"

"At this stage, in another ten days. The display will be moving on to France, to Baldwin's birthplace. Then it will journey home to Constantinople," she replied.

From the way his frown deepened, it was obvious George didn't like what he had heard.

Perhaps he was hoping it might remain in London for a little while longer.

Lady Alice leaned in and spoke to her husband. "Harry let's go into the last room and see the pieces in there. We should make room for the next guests. Thank you, Miss Scott. I never thought to see such an amazing relic from the crusader era. But if I'm honest about it, my feet hurt when I am on them for too long, so we mustn't tarry."

With the departure of Lord and Lady Steele, Jane found herself momentarily alone with George.

"And what of you, Miss Scott? Will you be leaving England with the crown or are you the one jewel that will be left behind?"

Jane narrowed her eyes at him. He had been quiet for most of the time, but George Hawkins had suddenly revealed himself to have quite the silver tongue. His easy smile set her on edge. "I shall be remaining in England for the foreseeable future, Mister Hawkins. But I am not certain of anything. I have learned through bitter experience that life doesn't wait for us to finish making plans."

He stepped closer; his gaze still fixed firmly on her. She caught a hint of his cologne. It was spicy. She liked it.

"Who knows, perhaps you and I may find ourselves travelling together somewhere on the road ahead." He gave one last brief glance at the crown before following his friends out of the room.

Jane remained behind; her heart slightly aflutter at how near he had come to her.

It had been a long time since a man had stood that close and made promises to Jane. Whispered sweet words that she had been a fool to believe. A life that should have been hers was now being lived by another woman.

What is done is done.

She wiped away a sudden tear and headed toward the

entrance. There was no time for grieving or regretting the past; she had more visitors to greet, a sultan to serve.

Reaching the front of the embassy, George's parting words slipped back into her mind. *You and I together somewhere on the road ahead.*

Jane frowned at the thought.

Could I ever trust a man again?

After Malta, she had been resolute that the days of placing her hopes and future in the hands of a man were behind her. But being all alone in the world made it a cold place for a young woman.

Even a friend would be a welcome respite from this lonely existence.

Chapter Five

George dropped into the overstuffed leather chair of his father's sitting room later that evening and let out a tired sigh. The night had not gone anywhere near according to plan. Instead of spending his time at the exhibition checking the embassy and its surrounds for likely ways to break in and steal the crown, he had made a fool of himself by staring all doe-eyed at Miss Jane Scott.

He pulled his notebook out of his jacket pocket and flipped it open. The scant notes sadly confirmed that he had indeed achieved little in the way of new knowledge of his intended goal.

"I didn't even write down the number of windows in the place. What is wrong with me?"

He was a professional thief. Someone held in high regard by his fellow criminals, yet here he had fallen under the spell of a woman. He ought to be ashamed of himself, but he couldn't muster up that emotion; especially not while his mind was focused almost completely on her.

You've met dozens of women, so what is it about Jane Scott that has you all flustered?

"I am flustered. I can't believe it," he muttered.

She was intriguing. Interesting. A breath of fresh air. All the things that most women of his acquaintance were not. He was drawn to her. The primal attraction unmistakable.

"Is this what Harry felt when he first met Alice? It's like a magnet, pulling you in."

George snapped the notebook shut. What a ridiculous notion. He was more than likely just caught off guard by the fact that the curator had turned out to be a female. His plans for bonding with J. Scott Esq. had been thrown for a loop—that was all.

There is not a hope in hell that I would let a woman get in the way of a job. Especially not when I only have ten days to carry it out.

Ten days. He was going to have to double down on his efforts in order to get his hands on the crown and spirit it away. This was a life-changing opportunity he couldn't afford to miss.

Vital minutes he should have spent making a clear assessment of the place had been wasted tonight. He hadn't a clue as to where the crown was stored after hours, nor the extent of the security arrangements, which were maintained by the embassy. Such amateur, stumbling missteps were totally foreign to him.

"You are an embarrassment to your craft."

His scattered thoughts found their way, yet again, to the brown-haired beauty. To those smokey, grey-green eyes.

Perhaps this evening wasn't a complete loss.

Not only was Jane Scott an attractive, young woman, but she had access to both the embassy and the crown. If he could find a way to strike up a friendship with her, he might be able to sweet-talk Jane into inadvertently revealing valuable information.

"Now that's an idea."

He would have to tread carefully. Any sort of connection

with her would need to be brief and over before he finished the job.

George winced at the thought. Being an outright cad didn't quite sit right, even for an unashamed rogue such as himself.

Just don't let her develop any emotional attachment to you and all will be right. Friendship is all you are offering.

He rose and headed over to the sideboard before pouring himself a stiff brandy. With his glass in hand, he settled back into the chair and picked up the notebook. A new plan began to form in his mind. By the time George had polished off his drink, he had filled several pages with detailed notes.

He finished the last sentence, then boldly underlined it. For a moment he sat and simply stared at what he had written.

Be charming. Be a gentleman.
Be bloody careful.

Chapter Six

❧

As she ushered the next lot of visitors into the exhibition the following evening, Jane did a double take. Trailing the rest of the group was a smiling George Hawkins.

"Mister Hawkins. This is an unexpected delight," she said.

He bowed his head. "I am here because I am ashamed to say that I didn't really pay much attention to the items on display last night. I was too distracted."

"Really? By what?" A ripple of heat coursed through her body as he drew close. Jane swallowed deeply.

His gaze flitted to the other guests then back to her. "By you, Miss Scott. First thing this morning, I paid a visit to a friend who I knew had a ticket for tonight and begged him to give it to me. When I told him about the intriguing young woman at the embassy, he immediately agreed."

Intriguing. He finds me interesting. Gosh. "I don't know what to say, Mister Hawkins. You have me at a loss." *You also have my full attention—even though I should know better.*

"Say you will come and walk with me in Hyde Park tomorrow afternoon. We can have tea and cake afterwards, and then I can escort you back here in time for the evening exhibition. That is unless of course you have family or personal commitments."

Jane caught the question in George's last remark. He was fishing, seeking to discover what family she might have in London. Or if she was in a relationship.

Perhaps there is one or two decent men in the world. And if I don't do anything foolish like risking my heart, what harm could come of it?

She would take a chance on George Hawkins. "No, I don't have any other obligations. An afternoon in Hyde Park would be lovely. Thank you, Mister Hawkins."

He bowed once more. "Excellent. Shall I call at your home?"

Jane shook her head. She liked George Hawkins, but she barely knew him. Now was not the time to reveal her current temporary living arrangements.

"Let's meet at the main entrance to Hyde Park at four o'clock. Now if you would excuse me, I had better get on with explaining the exhibition to the other guests."

He followed as she led the group into the second display room, making all the same oohs and ahhs as everyone else at the sight of Baldwin's crown. But unlike the other visitors, who clustered tightly together against the rope, George did as he had done the previous night and remained back from the group. It was almost as if he were taking in the whole scene rather than just the jeweled centerpiece.

Questions from several other interested patrons soon took her mind elsewhere, but whenever she got the chance, Jane would venture a glance in the direction of her new friend. More often than not, she found a pair of brown eyes staring back.

It was nice to be the subject of someone's interest—very nice indeed.

Chapter Seven

✦

"I don't think I could eat another thing for a month," said Jane.

George chuckled as she sat back in the chair and lay a hand over her belly. They had both just eaten two sizeable fruit buns. The cakes at this shop were particularly good, and he had chosen the place with her in mind. "My mother has been coming here every Thursday for seedcake and tea since I was a small boy, so I thought you might like it."

She grinned at him. "Your mother has excellent taste. I had forgotten how much I enjoyed the simple things, like good old plain English cooking. Though it is still a little odd to eat food without all those wonderful old-world spices."

George sat forward in his seat, eager to ask Jane more about her life in the east.

"How long did you and your family live in Byblos?"

He wanted to know as much as he could about Miss Jane Scott, but he was going to tread carefully—showing only the right amount of interest without raising any suspicions.

During their time as agents of the British crown, Stephen and Harry had taught George the subtle art of interrogation only too well. One never pressed hard for information. Rather, one set the most innocuous questions before a subject and then sat back and let them find a way to reveal everything about themselves.

Jane's gaze settled on her half-empty cup of tea, and she fell silent for a time. George could almost imagine her searching through her memories, sifting and sorting, before finally selecting the ones she felt comfortable enough to share with him. "We left England when I was eight. Mama, Papa, my brother, Michael, and myself. The first year we spent in Constantinople, and that was where my sister, Salma, was born. After that we moved to Byblos, and my father began to work on unearthing parts of the crusader castle. I was twenty-two by the time we finally left and set sail to come home to England."

"Which would explain your interesting and captivating accent," he replied.

She picked up her cup and took a slow sip. After placing it back on the saucer, Jane proceeded to pick nervously at the crumbs on her bread plate.

Don't push her. Let it go. She is already at the limit of what she wants to share.

"And what about you, George? Have you and your family always lived in London?"

Touché. That was a clever piece of diversion.

"Yes. I come from a family with a long history in the legal profession. Many of my forebears have been London-based judges. My father, of course, is disappointed that I didn't follow in his footsteps. Fortunately, my older brother, Richard, did, and that has kept the peace somewhat at home."

Jane wiped her face with her napkin. She lifted her gaze and met his once more.

"So, what exactly do you do for a living, George Hawkins?"

Oh, just the usual. I am a master thief with a penchant for jewels. In fact, I am currently working on finding a way to steal Baldwin's crown right from under your nose.

He cleared his throat. "I am an investor in a coaching business. My friends, including Lord Harry, started a company a year or so ago. We have three coaches now, with the view to further expansion in the near future."

The standard, boring company spiel that Monsale had taught them rolled easily off his tongue. It gave all the information someone would need, without inviting them to ask anything further.

"Coaches, you say. I would love to travel somewhere in England. Who knows? Now that I am back home, I may even become a customer of your business. I have always wanted to see Scotland." Again, she made no mention of her father, mother, or siblings, her words only being in regard to herself.

He was sorely tempted to ask her outright about the rest of the Scott family, but his deeply ingrained training held him back.

She sat upright in her seat and a forced, painted smile appeared on her lips. "Do you know where else I would like to go? Vauxhall. The pleasure gardens. I have heard so much about them. Tell me, are you a regular visitor?"

George hated Vauxhall with a passion. It was a din of pickpockets and larceny. If the thieves didn't get their hands on your wallet, their accomplices stole your precious coins at the card and dice games, which were always rigged.

Aside from the obvious downsides of the place, he was also not particularly keen to take Jane anywhere near that part of London. Vauxhall and Lambeth were where all his handlers of stolen goods just so happened to reside. If he set foot in the pleasure gardens with her, there was a good chance that one of his professional acquaintances would pop up and bid him a cheery hello.

And then what would I say? Miss Scott, may I introduce you to Mister Smith? He is what is known in the thieving trade as a fence. I am hoping he will get me a good price for Baldwin's crown which, if I haven't already mentioned, I am planning to steal.

"Vauxhall is dirty, crowded, and not much fun. And by the time the exhibition at the embassy is closed in the evening, all the special entertainments will be over," he lied.

Her face fell, and a hint of red appeared on her cheeks. "Oh, that's unfortunate."

Well done. Now you have made her sad.

He shouldn't care that she was disappointed. Jane Scott was supposed to be the means to an end. But even as she lifted her cup and downed the last of her tea, he couldn't just leave things as they were. "How about I take you for a late-evening stroll along the River Thames once you are finished tonight? We could get a bite of supper and perhaps a glass of wine somewhere," he said.

She set her empty cup down. "You don't have to do that, George. It was nice that you took me out this afternoon. I would hate for you to feel any sort of obligation toward me."

If he were an honorable man, a decent one, he would have regretted not offering to take her to Vauxhall. But George was a thief—the crown his goal.

Time to move in and work your charm, Georgie boy.

He reached across the table and touched his fingers softly to her right hand. "You have it all wrong, Jane. I was not being nice today because I felt obligated toward you. I am genuinely interested in getting to know you better. I like you." His gaze remained fixed on where their two hands were joined, on his thumb as it rolled gently across her knuckles.

When he touched the gold ring, with its honey-colored stone, which sat on her middle finger, she quickly pulled her arm back. "I . . . I like you too, George. But I think we should take this getting-to-know-one-another thing slowly and see where it leads."

Damn. She is too bloody lovely. And I am going to break this poor girl's heart.

But the thought that he was more than likely going to hurt Jane was still not enough for George to throw his plans away.

I want that crown.

Chapter Eight

It took all of Jane's strength not to shove the last of the straggling visitors out the front door of the embassy the following evening. The guard was about to close the door when she stopped him. "I have a friend arriving any minute now. Could you please wait until he is here?"

"Of course, Miss Scott."

She quickly turned on her heel and headed toward the display room. The ambassador was just placing the crown in its secure box when she arrived. "What a long night. I was beginning to think those people would never leave."

The ambassador nodded in the direction of the entrance, and heat raced to her cheeks as George walked into the room.

He bowed to them both before addressing Jane. "Good evening, Miss Scott. Will you be ready to leave soon?"

Doing her best to ignore the warmth on her face, Jane bowed to the ambassador. "*Sana iyi akşamlar diliyorum.*"

"And a good evening to you also, Miss Scott," he replied.

Once they were outside the embassy, George offered Jane his arm, and they headed down the path that ran along the riverbank.

"The ambassador seems a good man. Though I do find it

interesting that he is dressed in an English suit, rather than the traditional attire of his country," he said.

She nodded. "Yes. Mahmud the Second is looking to move his realm forward into the modern world. From what I understand, he plans to continue making extensive reforms throughout the Ottoman empire. Not that it hasn't been without its challenges or opposition. Having his foreign representatives dress like the men of their host countries is apparently all part of the plan."

They continued on along the Strand, eventually making their way to a small tavern close to the water's edge. It was neat and cozy. The moment they set foot through the door, George waved to the innkeeper and the man pointed to a booth at the back.

George slipped his hand in hers and guided Jane to an out-of-the-way, private table.

"I come here a bit, so the owner knows me," he explained.

Jane unbuttoned her coat and slid into the booth. After taking the seat opposite to hers, George waved over a tavern maid.

"Good evening, Mister Hawkins," she said, giving him a welcoming smile.

"Good evening. Could we please get a bottle of your good burgundy and two glasses? Oh, and a platter of supper things too. Thank you, Sarah," he said.

Jane found herself smiling at his easygoing nature. George Hawkins might well be the friend of lords and ladies, but he had a calm, comfortable way with people of all social classes. The barmaid certainly appeared to find him attractive.

I see I am not the only one who feels a little strange around him. Sarah clearly likes him too.

Jane waited until the tavern maid had left before finally daring to meet George's gaze. Her pulse quickened when he flashed a saucy little grin her way.

She liked what being this close to George did to her body.

He stirred sensations in her most secret of places and created a quiet yearning for his touch.

I wonder what sort of lover you would be with a woman like me. How adventurous could you make our time in bed? And would you ever let me take the lead?

※

He would give one hundred guineas for her thoughts. If the steamy look Jane was giving him across the table was anything to go by, George secretly imagined that her mind was filled with wicked, sexy ideas. But if she had the slightest inkling as to what biting on her bottom lip was doing to his hardening cock, she was keeping it to herself.

As far as you are concerned, she is an unwed woman and therefore out of reach. You don't meddle with innocents. She is also the person who stands between you and Baldwin's crown.

Though, if Jane climbed across the table and took him firmly in hand this very second, George might be tempted to give it all up. He could just picture her naked and beneath him.

"Here we are."

Shaken from his lustful fantasy, George sat back as the barmaid placed a large platter of food on the table between him and Jane. A second maid stepped up and handed George a bottle of wine.

Jane took the two glasses. "Thank you. This all looks wonderful."

George let out a slow breath as his manhood began to soften. "Yes, it does. They always serve excellent, fresh food here. Quite a few of the gentry come to this tavern, especially for their fried whitebait."

Jane's eyes grew wide. "Oh, yes. I do miss *Pulpetti tal-Makku*! They are the best thing in all of Malta."

Malta? "Sorry, what did you say?" he asked.

She chuckled. "Maltese whitebait fritters. You mix whitebait with eggs and some cheese, and you fry them in a pan with hot butter. They are heavenly."

When was she in Malta? That's part of the British Empire, not the Ottoman.

"I thought you said you lived on the far east coast of the Mediterranean, not on an island," he replied.

The look of joy on Jane's face disappeared, replaced by an unmistakable touch of sadness. "I was in Malta for two years. I returned to England just before Christmas at the end of last year."

Once again, she was only giving him scant information about her past. It bothered George greatly that Jane didn't appear willing to share private matters with him. It shouldn't, but it did.

She doesn't trust me. And can I blame her?

"And what have you been doing since you arrived back here? I mean, before this exhibition?" he asked.

Jane picked up a piece of bread and a slice of stilton cheese from the platter and took a bite. While she chewed her food, George sat silent. Finally, she let out a sigh, but she wouldn't meet his gaze. "I took on the role of a governess for a little while, just to make ends meet. On my days off, I usually went to the British Museum and spent my time going through the archives. I have a special interest in the English civil war. As did my father." She pointed toward the wine bottle. "May I?"

He poured them both a glass, then helped himself to some of the food.

As they sat quietly eating, George pondered the mystery that was Jane Scott. She was intelligent and well-read by the sound of it. Interesting, articulate women had always been attractive to him; the fact that she stirred his primal lust was an added bonus.

By the time they finished the wine, along with most of the food, and were making ready to leave, George had made up his mind.

I want that crown, but I also want her. Now I just have to figure out how I can make that happen.

Chapter Nine

❦

While it was a refreshing change to spend an evening with a gentleman, Jane still found herself constantly on edge. George was far too interested in her old life for her liking. The life she had spent the best part of a year trying to bury deep in her memory was not something she wished to discuss.

I am here to start afresh. To break free of the pain. Don't make me relive it.

As they left the tavern, George offered her his arm, and they began to head back toward the embassy. She quickly noted that the pace of his steps was slower than it had been on the walk over.

"Was the wine too much for you?" she ventured.

He shook his head. "No, I just want to spend as much time as I can with you. I hope that meets with your approval. If it doesn't, please say so."

She would be a fool to push away a friend. Lord knew she had been lonely since her return to England. Her mother's family lived somewhere in Scotland—she knew not where—and while her father's people kindly sent her a small annual

SASHA COTTMAN

stipend, they hadn't been particularly interested in actually reestablishing familial ties.

Loneliness was a hard and cold companion. Here was a living, breathing, and rather handsome man wishing to spend time with her.

I am taking a huge risk in getting involved with him. I should be focusing on finding the treasure, not gambling with my heart.

"I sense a reluctance on your part to open up to me, Jane. To trust," he said.

Jane nodded. She wasn't the least surprised that George could read her so well.

"I like being with you, George. You have to excuse me for being reticent at times. I don't trust easily. I have been burned before, and those were bitter lessons," she replied.

He stopped under a gas streetlamp, then drew in close. "Will you give me your trust now?"

She gazed into his eyes. The gold flecks in them promised so much.

I really want to believe that you like me. That someone in this world could find Jane Scott worthy of their affection.

"George, it would be lovely to openly trust you. But at some point, you must have realized that I have no one to protect me if you break your word," she said.

He paused for a moment, and his gaze dropped to the ground. A flicker of doubt appeared on his face, but when he raised his head and looked at her, it was gone.

Perhaps I imagined it.

"I won't betray you, Jane. You can trust me."

She gave him a brief nod, and he drew back.

They made their way toward the edge of the river, away from the other late-evening strollers. This time of the year, the nights were still warm, and the gentle breeze that blew up from the River Thames barely disturbed the air.

Fond memories stirred, returning to Jane like old friends. She was sure that if she closed her eyes and took a deep breath, she would be transported back to Byblos Castle and the heady, salt scent, of the sea as it swept up the hill each evening at sunset. Long, hot days, eased by the soothing cool night winds.

"Have you ever travelled abroad?" she asked.

"Yes, I go to France and Spain quite often. A friend of mine has a boat, and he brings various items into England from the continent. I also regularly go down to the coast to help him when he has a large shipment coming in."

Jane slipped her hand from George's and turned to face him. She barely knew this man, yet she wanted nothing more than to feel his strong arms wrapped tightly around her.

He reached out and drew her to him. It was almost as if he could read her mind. Their foreheads touched, and for just the briefest of moments, they stood in silence. The only sound breaking through into their private bubble was the gentle slap of waves dancing up and down in the nearby river.

"Jane, may I kiss you?" he whispered.

He could have taken what he wanted but knowing that he respected her enough to ask her permission had the last of Jane's crumbling defenses falling all around her. She couldn't fight the battle against her growing need any longer.

"Please," she murmured.

She lifted her face as George's lips brushed over hers. Once. Twice. And the third time, he claimed her mouth in a scorching kiss.

Yes. Oh, God, yes.

Her hands clutched the lapels of his coat. She was determined not to let go. When his left arm slipped around her waist and settled on her ass, she didn't protest. A sob of urgent need escaped her lips as he pulled her hard against him.

It's been an eternity since a man held me. Oh, George.

The firmness of his erection pressed into her stomach. For a fleeting moment, she wondered if he was going to back her up to a nearby tree and raise her skirts. She had a feeling she wouldn't stop him if he did. It had been so long.

When he finally did break away, they stood panting, staring at one another.

"You make me want to lose control. I've never met a woman who has had that sort of effect on me before. You might trust me, Jane, but I am not so certain that I can trust myself when it comes to you."

His words should have rung in her mind as a loud bell of warning, but Jane didn't care. She wanted to be a part of someone's life, even if only for a time. She tugged on the front of George's coat, pulling him in for another kiss.

I am tired of living in fear. Of wondering when the next heartache is coming.

Whatever this relationship was, and wherever it eventually led, Jane was going to take every minute she could get with George Hawkins.

Chapter Ten

Jane sipped at her tea and stared out into the night. Hope sat in her heart. Maybe, just maybe, her luck was beginning to change. The first tentative steps toward a possible romance were always fraught with danger, but if she could win George's heart, it would be worth the risk.

After setting her silver-etched tea glass onto the ornate gold tray, she tugged at the ties of her dressing gown. She shrugged it off and let it fall to the floor.

Her sensible, respectable, cotton English nightgown received a frown of disapproval. As her previous employment had required Jane to be able to attend immediately to her young charges at all hours, the dowdy night attire had been a necessary evil.

And since the ambassador's wife had kindly provided Jane with a maid, she was obliged to wear the gown while she sat and had her hair brushed each night.

She flicked open the top button, following quickly with the other two. It did little to reveal any skin, but she enjoyed these moments of private rebellion. With arms crossed in front, she grasped the sides of the garment and lifted it over her head. With a deft flick of her wrists, it joined the dressing gown on the floor.

"How do the women of this country ever get their men to touch them if they go to bed dressed like this?" she scoffed.

In the chill of winter, she could understand the need for something practical to keep her warm. Without the heat of a man's naked body, a girl could freeze. But it was early autumn, and the blankets on her bed were enough to keep out the chill of the night.

Much better.

In the privacy of her room, Jane could get away with being naked. She liked sleeping in the nude; the tactile sensation of the cool sheets against her skin heated her blood. She pulled back the covers, then climbed into bed.

Tonight, had been a challenge, then, to her a relief, a pleasant surprise. George had at first gently prodded Jane about her background, but he had retreated when she didn't give him any more than she was prepared to impart.

And I'm grateful he did.

If their relationship did move to another stage, then perhaps she would tell him of her life in Malta. Of her former lover.

The bedside candle was quickly snuffed out and she settled onto her back on the mattress. Her fingers brushed over her already peaked nipples, and she whispered, "George" as her hand slipped between her legs.

§

George peered up at the windows of the embassy from his hiding spot in the garden. After saying good night to Jane, and stealing another kiss, he'd walked away toward the Strand. A few minutes later, he'd returned and slipped in through the gate.

The light in an upper room went out. He shivered at the

memory of the art gallery. Never again would he risk creeping into a building so soon after the last candle had been extinguished.

Breaking into the embassy was not going to be an easy task. Unlike many other mansions and official residences in London, the Ottoman embassy faced straight onto the river. The front of the building had little in the way of gardens in which he could hide. There wasn't even a way to get around to the back, since the Adelphi buildings were all joined.

"Damn," he muttered.

The only way he was going to be able to break in was if he was already in the building when the doors were locked. The mere notion of a dangerous inside job made him nauseous.

Not a good idea allowing yourself to be hiding behind locked doors, George Hawkins. The hangman's noose is always waiting for fools who get too cocky.

If only Jane wasn't so honorable and respectable—he would be tempted to bring her into his plans. But he had already corrupted enough people during his life; he couldn't do that to a woman whose trust he was only just beginning to win.

Besides, he had a sneaking suspicion that Jane Scott wasn't the sort of woman easily swayed, especially not when it came to Baldwin's crown. The way she spoke with such reverence and respect for Sultan Mahmud, George was certain he would be a fool to suggest such a thing. She would be more than offended.

He turned on his heel and headed out onto the waterfront. A small boat was pulling up as he closed the gate silently behind him. The boatman jumped out of the vessel, rope in hand, and quickly tied it to a nearby iron cleat. He gave George a friendly nod as he passed by and moved toward a nearby tavern.

George looked back at the embassy. The answer to his monetary problems lay within. If he could get his hands on

Baldwin's crown; and either sell it as is or melt it down, he would have enough money to buy that fourth coach for the RR Coaching Company. Another coach that could bring enough real coin into the business, that he might finally be able to step back from his dangerous vocation.

He wouldn't have to steal any longer.

His fingers scratched the stubble on his chin as he pondered his dilemma. Stealing the crown would be a double-edged sword. He would have the money, but he doubted he would be able to keep Jane. The second the crown went missing, all hell would break loose.

And I so want her.

Jane and the whole staff of the Ottoman embassy would be searching everywhere trying to find whoever had stolen the crown. He couldn't risk being around when that happened. Couldn't risk getting caught.

George was torn between Jane and the priceless crown.

That had always been your plan. You were just stupid enough to start to feel something for the chit. When did you ever mix business with pleasure?

Stuffing his hands into his coat pockets, he began the slow walk home to Argyle Street. There was nothing else he could do tonight. A hard choice would have to be made. If he wanted the money, which the treasured jewel could bring, he was going to have to betray Jane.

Chapter Eleven

❧

Jane ran her hands over the front of her gown once more. There wasn't a crease or mark on it, but she was nervous. It was the first time she had been to a private dinner at a home since her return to London. A dinner where a duke and other nobles would be present.

She checked herself in the mirror. Hair brushed to within an inch of its life. White blouse as bright as the sun. And a burgundy silk skirt with a matching bodice that lifted her breasts perfectly. It was one of the few remaining items of clothing still in her possession from when her mother had gone shopping just before they left Constantinople on their ill-fated journey home.

"They will have to take me as I am," she said to her reflection.

It was her best gown. The one she wore for meeting important people. For making the very best of impressions. The elegant black embroidery at the top of the bodice was always a conversation starter.

I hope they take me as I am. It would be nice to make some real friends.

She picked up her evening cloak, then headed downstairs

to where Lord Harry Steele's private carriage was waiting out the front of the embassy.

As the coach slowed to a halt at an address in Grosvenor Street a short time later, she reached for the door handle. Her fingers had barely touched it when the door suddenly opened, and George's smiling face appeared. "I was beginning to worry that you might have changed your mind and not come."

"No, I was delayed getting something finalized at the embassy," she replied.

Or, more truthfully, I took forever to get dressed and spent the last hour practicing what I would say to your friends.

Friday being the holy day of the week for the Muslim faith meant the exhibition at the Ottoman embassy was closed, and Jane was afforded a rare day off. With only three days remaining in which, they could catch a glimpse of Baldwin's crown, the London crowds had been hectic to say the least. The invitation to dine with Lord and Lady Steele this evening had been a delightful and welcome surprise.

George helped her down from the carriage, after which Jane nervously inspected her clothes once more.

He leaned in and brushed a kiss on her cheek. "You look wonderful. And don't be shy around my friends; they are really looking forward to spending an evening with you."

Their gazes met, and a now familiar heat coursed through Jane's body. After that kiss at the riverbank, George had wasted no time in stealing as many of them as he could. His attentions were wonderful. She felt more alive than she had done since leaving Malta.

He also came to the embassy every evening, waiting until all the other visitors had left before spending time with her. She couldn't have a gentleman caller in her room, so they usually took the short walk down to the river where they indulged in long, luxurious embraces before he escorted her back to the main display room and then took his leave.

Each evening, she found herself searching the milling crowd for George's familiar, handsome face, her heart giving a little skip when she caught sight of him.

There was no doubt in her mind. She was surely falling in love with him—and it worried her.

If it had been another man, the prospect of a new romance would have filled her with joy, but with George, Jane still found herself holding back a little.

Matters between them were moving quickly, leading her at times to ponder the question as to why. There was something about the irresistible rogue that still had her unsure as to his motives. The peculiar look that appeared on his face whenever George gazed at Baldwin's crown set her nerves on edge.

"George why am I here tonight?" she asked.

He gifted her with one of his easy smiles. "Because I want you to get to know my friends. And if I am honest, they want to hear more about your life in the Ottoman Empire. Oh, and, of course, more about Baldwin's crown."

You said you would trust him.

But that was easier said than done.

※

The evening's social event had not been in George's plans. But once Alice discovered that he had been spending time with Jane Scott, she had insisted on issuing an invitation for Jane to dine with them at the mansion in Grosvenor Street. Harry had also extended the invite to the rest of the rogues of the road. By the time George had heard about the dinner party, it was all too late to do anything about it.

Fortunately, lady's man Augustus Jones was somewhere off the coast of France onboard his yacht *The Night Wind* and therefore unable to attend. And as for Sir Stephen Moore—his movements of late had been at the very least, suspect. Apart from when he was at the coaching company offices with Toby, who was currently asleep upstairs, he was rarely to be seen. Much as he would love to know what was going on with Stephen, George knew better than to go poking into the private affairs of one of his fellow rogues.

So that left George, Harry, Alice, Jane, Monsale, and Harry's sister, Lady Naomi Steele, on the dinner party guest list.

George led Jane into the elegant cream-painted mansion, and after helping her out of her cloak, handed it to a nearby footman.

His gaze ran appreciatively over the fitted burgundy bodice of Jane's gown. Unlike the other dull, grey creations she normally wore, this one favored her generous breasts, displaying them to their best advantage.

I would love to get my hands on those. Naked and ready for my lips.

He gritted his teeth, angry with himself.

No. You can't be thinking like that when it comes to her. This having-an-emotional-attachment-to-Jane nonsense must stop. It isn't right.

"Miss Scott, what a delight. I am so glad you could make it tonight," said Alice.

George took a respectable step back as their hostess came to greet her guest. Alice Steele held out her hands and drew a blushing Jane into a hug.

"Aren't I supposed to be curtsying to you?" said Jane.

Alice laughed. "No, most definitely not. I wasn't born a noble. My father is in textiles and shipping. I'm what you call 'new money.'"

Harry appeared at her side and slipped his arm partway around his wife's waist. His other hand rested protectively on her baby belly. He pressed a tender kiss on her cheek. "My wife is more noble than the rest of us put together. Now come. Let's eat. I am starving."

As they stepped into the dining room, George caught sight of the two other guests: Monsale and Lady Naomi Steele. They appeared to be having some sort of heated disagreement, but quickly drew apart as everyone else arrived. Naomi gave the duke a haughty huff then hurried over to Jane. Monsale shook his head and followed in Naomi's wake.

Harry met George's gaze and scowled. As Jane was his friend, it was up to George to make the introductions.

I just wish you weren't all so friendly and welcoming to her. This will only make things that more difficult when the time comes.

George was now regretting not having told his fellow rogues of the road about his plans to steal the crown. Secrecy was usually his best professional tool, but in this case, it was fast becoming a liability.

"Your grace, may I present Miss Jane Scott. Jane, the Duke of Monsale," he said.

Monsale gave Jane a chin tip—his usual curt method of greeting women. "Miss Scott, welcome."

George was about to introduce Lady Naomi, but she pushed past him and took a hold of Jane's arm. "Jane. May I call you Jane? Oh, good. Thank you. Now I want to hear all about life in the Ottoman Empire. It must be so much more interesting than dull old London."

And that was pretty much how the rest of the evening went. George was left to talk business with Monsale and Harry while the women sat giggling over the rumors of what went on in the sultan's harem.

"George, how are you going with securing funds for that proposed service through to Oxford? I think if we can get a new coach and driver, we could pick up some of the university student traffic. That route is a lucrative one we should be exploiting," said Monsale.

"I am working on it," replied George.

He stole a glance at Jane as he spoke. She was engrossed in a conversation with Lady Naomi, her eyes sparkling with mirth at some shared jest. As he took in the sight, the last remnants of George's good humor flittered away.

I am a dreadful man. I don't deserve a shot at a good life.

By the time a footman placed a large platter of fillet of roast pork in the middle of the table at the start of the second course, George had all but lost his appetite.

"Jane, how much longer is the Ottoman exhibition in London? I hear it has been exceptionally popular," said Alice.

Jane dabbed at her face with her napkin. "It comes to a close in the next few days. We did extend it for a little longer, but with commitments in France, the items will have to leave England by mid next week."

George picked up his wine glass and took a generous sip. The clock was ticking loudly on his plans to steal the crown.

"And will you be accompanying the items when they travel to the continent?" asked Lady Naomi.

George waved over a nearby footman, suddenly not wishing to consider what life would be like for Jane after he made a move to steal the crown.

What if they try and blame her for the theft?

"I will not. I shall be seeking a new position somewhere in London. The exhibition will eventually return to Constantinople, and I have no reason to go with it," she replied.

"Don't you have family to return to in the east?" asked Alice.

"No. No family."

George pointed at the pork, sitting back in his chair intently watching while his plate was filled with meat and roasted vegetables. The last thing he wished to do was to look at Jane. He was convinced that if he did, she would see the wicked intentions which he was certain were written all over his face.

The footman worked his way around the table, serving each guest in turn. When he reached Jane, she took one look at the pork and waved it away. "No, thank you."

"It's good; you should try a piece. Our cook is particularly skilled at making roast meat juicy and tender," offered Harry.

A tight smile appeared on her lips. "Pork is forbidden by the Quran, and I haven't eaten it since I was a child. And even if I did eat it, today is a holy day; it would not be respectful of me to go back to the Ottoman embassy after having partaken. So, I must politely decline."

George inwardly sighed. Jane Scott was not only intelligent and beautiful, but she had a moral compass. She had honor and dignity.

He pushed his plate away, no longer able to face his food. If he had a soul to feed, it would already be stuffed full to the brim with shame.

At the end of the evening, a grim-faced George escorted Jane out into Grosvenor Street and to the Steele family carriage. He opened the door, then held out his hand to her.

She didn't take it. "Thank you for this evening, George. I had a lovely time. Your friends are wonderful people."

When he gave an almost absent-minded nod in response to her words, Jane reached for George's arm.

"You have been in a dour mood for the best part of an hour. Did I say something wrong?" she said.

He wouldn't meet her gaze.

"It's not you; it's me. You were perfect this evening, Jane. But I am not feeling the best. I suspect I am coming down with something."

That explains why he didn't finish his meal.

"Is there anything I can do?" she offered.

George shook his head. "No, thank you. Just go home."

Jane dampened her disappointment over the way the evening was ending. Her hopes for a good night kiss or two evaporated at hearing George's lackluster words.

"If you are still unwell tomorrow, then send word. I am sure we can survive one night without seeing one another. I hope a good night's sleep restores you."

After climbing into the carriage, Jane waited for George to close the door.

He stood gazing at the pavement for a moment, then finally lifted his head and met her gaze. "Good night, Jane," he said, and pushed the door shut. He turned and walked straight back into the house.

As the carriage pulled away from the side of the street, Jane stared at George's retreating form. A hollow sensation sat in her stomach.

Why did that sound like goodbye?

Chapter Twelve

George stopped a few hundred yards short of the Ottoman embassy and sat his ass on the step of a closed drapery shop. Twice already on the way over from Argyle Street, he had almost given up and gone home.

It was one of the few times in his long and dishonorable career as a master thief that he found himself having second thoughts about a job. Serious second thoughts.

With hands clenched tightly into fists, he grappled with the decision that was before him. His life could fundamentally change on the toss of a coin.

If he backed away from stealing the crown, he had a chance at a future with Jane. He could openly offer her his heart. She wouldn't have to go back to being a governess.

"No, she would be the wife of a near penniless second son of a judge. A man who handles stolen goods for a living," he muttered.

He could just imagine how well that would go down with her.

If Jane had any sense, she would get on that ship and go back to Constantinople along with Baldwin's crown. She would be safe from a blackguard like me.

But if he screwed his courage to the sticking place and went through with snatching the ancient jeweled treasure, he could finally get out from under his life of thievery and disgrace. He would still never be able to look his father fully in the eye, but he could follow in Harry's footsteps and turn over a new leaf.

He got to his feet, brushing off the dust from the back of his jacket.

"I don't deserve a good, honest woman like Jane Scott. I am a criminal through and through."

George Hawkins headed for the Ottoman embassy and his fate.

George knew the layout of the exhibition space well enough. There were two slightly disinterested embassy guards usually loitering about the place. Every so often one or both would disappear outside to smoke some tobacco, leaving the main public area largely unprotected.

Their lack of care in their job was his way in.

Tonight, he avoided Jane. He told himself it was purely for strategic reasons, but a little voice inside his head whispered *coward*.

She was somewhere in the next room showing the last of the visitors the gold crown when George slipped in the front door. He passed the guards on his way through the entrance. They had their backs turned to him and were chortling over a magazine that one of them was holding.

He stifled a snort. Sketches of naked women had universal appeal for all men.

There was little over half an hour remaining in the opening hours of the exhibition, and George wasted no time in making his way to the hiding place he had carefully selected. On any other night, he would soon be arriving and making his presence known to Jane. Tonight, however, he couldn't risk her coming out to the entrance and looking for him.

He had feigned the beginnings of a cold at the end of the previous evening, and hopefully she would think he had taken to his bed rather than pass it onto her.

To one side of the first room there was a doorway, and after checking that he wasn't being observed, George made his way through it and into a narrow hallway. He quickly looked left and right.

Good. No one is here. It's all coming together. Just hold your nerve.

Three days earlier he had identified the place where he would hide and come out once everyone had gone. His trusty skeleton key made short work of the door to the broom closet.

He closed the door and moved to the back where he soon settled on the floor in the far corner. Under a convenient, holland cover he was hidden entirely from view. Anyone who chanced to come into the cramped room in the next hour would only see brooms, buckets, and a pile of cloths.

In the dark, George sat and waited. Not long now and he would be able to make his move. He talked to himself as he often did during the long waiting periods before undertaking jobs. Tonight, he made a vow.

After this is done, I will go straight. No more stealing. No more lying.

The promise did little to appease his soul, because with the golden crown of Emperor Baldwin in his possession, there would be no more Jane.

He would have his new life, but it would come at a high price.

Chapter Thirteen

Under the heavy cover, George was cramped and hot. Someone had used it to wipe up something foul and rotten. He sniffed at the sleeve of his coat.

I don't know what that awful stuff is, but I will never be able to get it out of this fabric. My coat, my shirt—everything is tainted with it.

He consoled himself with the knowledge that if he did manage to pull the job off, he would have enough money to treat himself to several new coats and suits. Once he got home, he would indulge in a long, hot bath and scrub the smell out of his pores.

No. A bathhouse might be a better option. Dump the crown somewhere safe and then go and have a wash.

The last thing he needed was for the Hawkins household staff to make comments about the stench of his clothes and for his parents to enquire as to where he had been.

Settling in for a long wait, George did his best to endure the odoriferous pong.

I knew I should have packed a hipflask for this.

An hour after the last of the visitors were scheduled to have left the building, George finally opened the door of the closet and stepped out. The hallway was dark, but at least the full moon was shining through an upper window.

Studying the phases of the moon was something all good thieves did as a matter of good business practice. A full moon often allowed for dirty work without the need of a lantern or candle.

With slow, soft footsteps, he crept through the main entrance and into the first display room. He stopped and listened. Silence was his reward.

He moved on, and into the second space where Baldwin's crown was usually displayed. His heart was beating like a drum in his chest as his gaze took in the ornate storage box, which had been placed on the top of the dais.

Bloody fools. You think too highly of the English. I would have thought after Elgin took all those beautiful marbles from Athens that you would have learned we are not above petty theft.

He might not think too much of the embassy's attempts at security, but he was pleased they had already gift-wrapped the crown. All he had to do was pick up the box and make his way out the front door to where the Thames River boatman he had bribed was waiting.

In a matter of minutes, both he and the crown would be gone—sailing down the river and well away from here.

Stepping up to the box, he ran his fingers over its gilt covering. If his luck held, he might be able to get a good price for the melted-down silver in some distant market in France.

"Come on, my beauty. It's time to leave."

CLICK.

George's blood turned to ice at the unmistakable sound of a pistol being cocked.

"Hands up, then slowly turn around. No false moves or I will scream the place down."

The gun was bad enough but knowing who was holding it tore a hole through George's heart. He had betrayed her. The consequences of his shameful deed were now to be faced. There was no doubt he would pay a hefty price.

Bloody. Bollocks. Buggery. Oh!

He knew better than to argue with anyone holding a loaded and set pistol. With hands raised, George spun unhurriedly on the heel of his boot and faced Jane.

Their gazes met, and he offered up a sultry smile.

"Why would you scream if you are holding a weapon?" George silently cursed the tremble in his voice.

All the times he'd imagined being caught stealing; he had pictured himself as being braver.

"Because if I did, every person in this place would come running. And you would be flat out of luck. As it is, you only have me to deal with, but I assure you I am a crack shot," she replied.

He took a step toward her, half-confident that if she had wanted to shoot him, she would have done so by now.

I bloody well hope so, otherwise this could end very badly for me.

Jane having him arrested might well be the least of George's problems.

His hands dropped, and Jane tsked. "Don't do that, George. Put your hands right up in the air please."

Another of his steps was followed by a third. There was little more than a yard between them now. Three or so feet before he could get his hands on the pistol. "You won't shoot me. Let's not be foolish about this."

She waved the pistol in the air, then aimed it at his chest. "What makes you think I won't pull the trigger?"

He risked another step, then stopped. George might well have a gambler's heart, but he wasn't completely stupid. Loaded pistols had a nasty tendency of going off, and he didn't want to be in the firing line if this one did. "I don't think you will shoot, because this is me. You like me." George swallowed deeply, doing his best to ignore his racing heart.

Jane let out a ragged breath and lowered the pistol. "I am well past the point of just liking you, George. But I think you might already know that you deceitful blackguard. I wish to God I didn't have feelings for you. I sensed you were trouble from the outset. Last night, you pretended to be falling ill, but I wasn't fooled. When you didn't show earlier this evening, I knew you were going to finally make a move."

"I didn't want to hurt you."

I wish you could believe that, because it is the truth. I never wanted you mixed up in my terrible life.

"I know I am a rogue, but you love me, and isn't that all that matters? Tell me the truth of your heart, Jane, and we can sort this out. We can be together."

He moved closer.

Jane took a step back and raised the weapon once more. There were tears glistening in her eyes, but her hand was steady. "The truth is you are a liar and a thief."

She was going to turn him in to the authorities. The hangman's noose beckoned. There was nothing else for it, but to take the risk.

Forgive me.

With one hand, George reached for Jane—the other went for the pistol.

There was a loud bang and a puff of smoke. Searing pain shot through him. George glanced down at his white shirt and the crimson stain which was rapidly spreading across the front of it.

"You bloody well shot me!"

His world turned black.

Chapter Fourteen

Two weeks later

George put down the book he was reading when Alice stepped into the room. As she approached, she gave him one of her trademark filthy looks. Angry pregnant women were surprisingly fearsome creatures.

"You have a visitor," she said.

He shifted in the chair, attempting to find a more comfortable spot. His wound protested, and he winced. He got a 'serves you right' glance in reply from Alice as she turned and headed out the door.

Sympathy for his injury had evaporated long ago in the Steele household, but George was in no position to complain. Alice and Harry were keeping him hidden from the rest of London society, and most importantly . . . the law.

George was sitting in the main drawing room on the second floor of 16 Grosvenor Street. He dared not go home. Explaining a bullet wound to his father was beyond even George's extensive skills of lying. Instead, a note had been sent mentioning him taking a sudden and lengthy trip to France on Gus's boat.

"You could at least tell me who my visitor is?" he called after Alice.

"It's me."

George stilled as Jane walked into the room, a brown leather satchel slung over her shoulder. He eyed her warily, remembering the outcome of their last encounter.

She held up her hands. "Rest easy. I am not carrying any hidden weapons. I come in peace."

"That's a bit late, don't you think? Considering that you've already shot me," he replied.

She waved his comment away as she casually dropped into the chair opposite him and crossed her legs. There was something different in her demeanor from the Jane he thought he knew.

She unhooked the satchel and set it on the floor. "Yes, but I did bring you here and made sure that your attempt to steal a priceless ancient artifact did not become public knowledge. You should be thanking me for having avoided a serious international incident."

It was clear he wasn't going to get an ounce of compassion, let alone an apology from Jane. "Remind me to thank you when I am able to move again without pain."

For the first time since she had entered the room, the expression on Jane's face softened. She leaned forward and rested a hand on his knee. "How are you?"

"Tired. Sore. And still trying to figure out why you bloody well put a bullet in my shoulder."

A flash of pain crossed her face, and guilt pricked him sharply. Her look reminded him that he had not been the only one hurt that night.

"I shot you because you deserved it. You used me in order to steal Baldwin's crown. Just be grateful I didn't aim for your balls."

Memories of that moment came rushing back to him—sharp pain and shock, then falling and darkness. He saw snippets of images of Harry. More pain. Worried faces staring down at him. The gruff voice of a doctor. Then the blessed relief of laudanum. And finally, nothing.

"How did you get me out of the embassy? I haven't quite figured that part out," he said.

"You mean why are you not sitting languishing in a prison cell? I hauled you out into the street and hailed a hack. And may I make mention that you are not a small man, and your unconscious body was like trying to drag an elephant. Fortunately, when we got here, Harry carried you inside and Alice sent for a surgeon. Apparently, you and your friends have a standing relationship with several medical professionals, and one came at short notice."

George's anger toward Jane cooled. She had risked a great deal in helping him escape. After the way he had betrayed her trust, he was genuinely surprised that she hadn't summoned the rest of the embassy staff and had him clasped in irons.

A knock at the door preceded a footman carrying a tray with a teapot, cups, and a plate of small cakes. He set them on a nearby side table, then stepped back. "Mister Hawkins, Lord Harry asked me to inform you that he has received legal advice and the offer is sound. And as for Lady Steele, she said to give you the following message." He nervously cleared his throat. "Don't be a bloody idiot." He gave a curt bow then left the room. The door hadn't quite closed before the footman's dirty chuckle drifted to George's ears.

Cheeky beggar.

His mood was not improved by the sly grin which now sat on Jane's lips. It was clear that even his friends had taken her side.

"What does Alice mean by 'don't be an idiot?'" he asked.

Jane uncrossed her legs and lifted the satchel onto her lap.

After a brief moment of rummaging around, followed by the rustle of papers, she produced an old, tattered folio. "Before I explain what all this means, there is something I need to get off my chest."

George nodded. If the shoe had been on the other foot, he wouldn't have strolled so calmly into the room. He couldn't blame Jane if her intentions included tearing strips off him.

"I have come to the realization that while you were toying with my emotions and letting me develop a sense of romantic attachment to you, you were, in fact, planning on betraying me. Do you have the slightest notion as to how much that hurts?"

"If I said yes, would you believe me?" he replied.

"No. Because I have also come to the heartbreaking understanding that you, George Hawkins, are nothing more than a ruthless criminal. I am still in two minds as to whether I should report you to the authorities and let them deal with you."

He held up his hand. "I fully—"

"No! You don't," she interjected.

Jane leaned forward in the chair and pointed her finger at him. "It took years of diplomatic moves to get Baldwin's crown to England, for the sultan to agree to let it leave Constantinople. So, I am bloody well certain that you don't have the foggiest of notions as to how hard it would have been for me to tell the ambassador that someone had stolen it from under his nose." Tears sparkled in her eyes.

He hadn't just betrayed her; he had broken her heart. "You're right. I don't know what this has cost you. All I can say is that two weeks of bed rest has given me time to reflect on a few things. One of which is that I have to become a better man, to turn my life around."

"Is that your version of an apology?" The pain underlying her accusation was clear.

As far as she was concerned, he had no idea what he had

done to her. And if she thought him clueless, how could he have any chance to make amends?

If I could just hold you in my arms and tell you that I am so sorry for everything I did to you. That I will do anything to have you believe in me again. Oh, Jane. What sort of fool would choose a jewel over something as precious as you?

"Because if it is, then I may as well give up now and leave. A man who thinks that a brief 'sorry' is enough, doesn't deserve a second chance at anything."

"Jane I am so sorry for what I did. I hate that those words sound trite and hollow, but I am sorry. More than you can ever know. Please believe me when I say, I have much to atone for—not the least being that I stole your love."

He had been reckless and selfish. And it had cost him dearly. But George Hawkins was still a rogue, and he was determined that what had once been his would be his again.

I don't care what it takes. I want you back. I want you forever.

"I know you might hate me at this juncture, and with good reason, but I am not giving up on us."

She glared at him. "You flatter yourself, George Hawkins. As far as I am concerned, there is no *us*; and I only mentioned a sense of romantic attachment. You were the one who used the word love."

Chapter Fifteen

She shouldn't derive any sort of pleasure in seeing him so awkward and ashamed, but Jane did. It had taken all her resolve not to shoot him a second time that night, or to scream bloody murder and turn him over to the authorities.

He had stolen something of great value from her.

And yet you are still in love with the scoundrel.

Her gaze settled on the satchel, and with some effort she forced her heartache down. She wasn't here to rehash the events of what had happened at the embassy or even the tender moments they had shared in the days leading up to it.

"You will be pleased to know that Baldwin's crown has safely left England and is now on display in Flanders. It will then travel onto Paris and finally Valenciennes, Baldwin's birthplace, before returning home to Constantinople."

With the exhibition over, she was back to seeking a new position as well as somewhere to live. The Ottoman ambassador was a kind man, but she could only remain at the embassy for a little while longer before she outstayed her welcome.

"Which means that I am now at a loose end. And this is

where *you* step back into the story, and hopefully redeem yourself," she said.

"Yes?"

Jane took a deep breath and steadied her nerves. She had rehearsed the words enough times to her reflection in the mirror, but actually saying them to George in person was a different matter.

"I want you to buy me a house. If you don't, I will have you arrested."

※

George did a double take. He knew the smell and taste of blackmail only too well. He just hadn't expected to hear it come from her.

He was still trying to absorb the shock of her demand when the door opened and through it walked Alice and Harry.

"Has he agreed to help?" asked Harry.

"Not yet. I think poor George might be in shock," replied Jane.

A grinning Alice raised an eyebrow in George's direction. "She is good. In fact, she reminds me very much of myself. Brains and beauty, but with a spine of steel."

Harry turned his back, and from the snorts and trembling of his shoulders, it was obvious he wasn't making much of an effort not to laugh.

Bastard.

Alice and Harry quickly made themselves comfortable on a nearby sofa, pouring cups of tea and offering cake all around.

George glared at Harry when he put a seedcake under his nose. "Thank you, no."

With a sigh, Jane opened the folio and handed George a piece of paper. "Read it," she said.

. . .

There is one way possible that you may get a swiving from me ... you must excuse my plain expressions ... you may be conveyed into the stool-room which is within my bedchamber while I am at dinner; by which means I shall have five hours to embrace and nip you.

George frowned and quickly handed the note back. "I don't know what this is, apart from the obvious. It's some old letter offering to have a sexual liaison with someone. What could that possibly have to do with you demanding that I buy you a house?"

Jane grinned at him. "It's a letter written by King Charles the First to his mistress, Jane Whorwood. A letter that for many years was considered to only exist in fanciful legend. But my father believed in it, as did I. It took me many months to locate the original coded letter at the British Museum, and just as many to find the cypher to unlock its message."

George's heart began to race. As his excitement rose, he suddenly understood why the tea had been brought in. His mouth was dry and parched. "Go on."

Alice clapped her hands together in unrestrained delight, but Jane still held his attention. "My father also believed in the treasure that my namesake was supposedly given by the King before his unfortunate execution. A treasure that has remained a secret for nearly one hundred and seventy years, along with its location."

George was enraptured. "And you think the letter might hold a clue?"

"During the English civil war, Jane Whorwood moved secretly about England and at times the continent, all the while helping to smuggle funds for the King in his battle against the parliamentarian forces of Oliver Cromwell. What no one knew was exactly *where* she stayed in London. Or where the treasure might be buried."

Jane tucked the letter back into the folio and then closed the satchel. She got to her feet. "Do you feel well enough for a short walk?"

The air in the room was electric with expectation. George still didn't fully understand why Jane and the others were telling him about the letter and the hidden treasure, but he found himself fully invested. "Please tell me you have found where Jane Whorwood lived."

She motioned to the door. "Get your coat. I am going to show you the house, and then you are going to buy it for me."

Chapter Sixteen

It was little over a mile from 16 Grosvenor Street to 11 Coal Yard Lane, but it could have been a world away such was the difference between the two addresses. While Harry and Alice's fine mansion was elegant and spotlessly clean, the house which Jane stopped out the front of was dirty and rundown.

Jane met George's questioning gaze. "I will grant you that it is not a nice part of town. I don't expect that even in King Charles's day it would have been particularly attractive real estate, but that is the beauty of it. No one would ever come looking for a king's secret mistress in such a hovel."

He stared at her for a moment. Alice was right in her assessment of Jane Scott. She was a woman in possession of a sharp mind and steady nerves. And he had been a fool to pretend otherwise.

And to think I betrayed you. I am an idiot.

"Come on." Jane led him to a shop several doors down from the house, the outside of which was black with years of filth and smoke. As they stepped through the doorway, George discovered, to his disgust, that inside was no better.

Behind a long, dusty counter stood the shopkeeper. In

front of him sat several loaves of what appeared to be moldy bread. Some poor soul was going to pay good money to buy that food, and then eat it.

He shuddered at the thought.

I can't believe that man has the hide to sell rotten food.

The shopkeeper wiped his hands on his filthy, stained apron and considered them both. He gave Jane a salacious smile, which made George's already offended stomach churn.

"Ah, so you are back. Thought I might be seein' you again. And this time you bought a gentleman wiv you. Is he your pimp? And does he have any coin?" said the shopkeeper.

If I didn't have a bullet wound in my shoulder, you would be picking your teeth up off the floor.

To George's surprise and utter dismay, instead of Jane taking offence, she simply smiled at the man.

What the devil?

She leaned over the counter, not flinching when the shopkeeper's gaze drifted to her breasts. George was ready to commit murder if the man so much as moved his hand in the direction of Jane's body.

"Who he is and what coin he has will depend on whether you are going to let me have another look at the house," she said.

When the shopkeeper winked at Jane, George was on the verge of ignoring his injured arm and throwing a punch or two at the man's head. Jane, however, seemed more than happy to continue to toy with him.

She smiled sweetly once more at the shopkeeper as he handed over a set of keys.

"Thank you, darling," she said, and blew him a kiss.

Outside in the street, George couldn't hold either his tongue or temper any longer. He rounded on Jane. "What on earth was that all about? You were flirting with him. Have you no self-respect?"

Jane raised an eyebrow. "Not that it's any of your business, but my sweet-talking of men like him has been getting me plenty of discounts and special favors all over London. You are not the only one who has the gift of a silver tongue, George Hawkins. I was raised alongside the local market children in Byblos, and they could negotiate you into the dust." She waved the key in his face, then turned and headed toward number eleven. A still thoroughly displeased George followed.

When they reached the house, he took a hold of the corner of her coat sleeve. "I don't think you realize the risk you are running in playing games with a man like him. I know his kind. The minute he thinks he can take advantage of you he will."

Jane stopped a few feet shy of the front door. She turned and roughly brushed George's hand away. "I am not the innocent you seem to think I am, George. The world is full of men seeking to take what they can from young, vulnerable women. I include you in that list. Believe me, I don't fully trust anyone. I made that mistake once before, and I will be damned if I will ever do it again."

While Jane jingled the set of keys in her hand, a sheepish George set his gaze to the upper levels of the house and other nearby buildings. Anything to avoid having to meet her eyes. "This place needs to be condemned and torn down," he muttered.

The façade of the house reminded him of the RR Coaching Company offices in Gracechurch Street. Alice had made plenty of noises about painting the building and making it more enticing for potential customers, but Monsale wouldn't have it. To his way of thinking, the dingy look kept prying eyes away. And initially, George had agreed.

But the time will come when it will need a tart up. If we are ever going make an attempt to run an honest business, we have to be able to attract paying customers.

Jane fiddled with the lock for a moment, wriggling it back and forth.

Finally, George stepped up and held out his hand. "May I? You might have the gift of a smile for getting things done, but keys and locks are somewhat of a specialty for me."

She gave him a filthy look, then took a step back. Within seconds, George had the door open.

The instant he set foot inside the three-storied ramshackle house, the stench of years of neglect and filth assaulted his senses. George winced. "This is almost as bad as the foul cloth under which I hid for an hour at the embassy."

She patted him on the back. "Yes, but this one doesn't come with the added pain of a bullet."

He glanced at her. This was the first time since Jane had arrived at Grosvenor Street earlier that morning that she appeared to have lowered her guard with him. It wasn't much, but it was a start.

"Why does the shopkeeper think you are on the game?" he asked.

She screwed up her face. "Would you judge me harshly if I told you that I may have led him to form that opinion? I was hardly going to knock on the man's front door and tell him I was in search of hidden treasure that may just happen to be in a house that he currently owns. He has to believe that I have a good reason to want to come and live in this rat-infested hellhole."

Of course. That makes sense. I think last night's dose of laudanum might have addled my mind.

"I doubt I could ever find you wanting for character," he replied.

Jane reached past George and pushed the front door closed. "The reality is that there are few people who would offer him any sort of money for this shabby mess. And they are more than likely the sort to be engaged in less than moral occupations." She shook her head. "I am surprised I am having to explain that to you, George."

He flinched. No one had ever called him out on his nefarious ways, and to hear Jane say such a thing actually stung. If it had been one of the other members of the rogues of the road who had accused him of being wicked, he might have managed to laugh it off. But it was different with Jane. With her, he didn't feel the same sense of levity about being a career criminal.

His view of Jane was in constant flux. She was clearly not some innocent miss. How much she did know of the world and the truth of life was a question George badly wanted answered.

He followed her farther inside the house, and at the end of a short hallway they stepped into a basic kitchen. Jane stopped and held out her hands, presenting the space to him. "What do you think? If you ask me, I can just imagine how perfect it will be for when we start a family. A baby's crib would look lovely in the corner."

George's blood turned to ice. He hadn't even got to the point of considering the possibility of one day settling down, let alone starting a family. And here Jane was, already picking out where furniture would go.

Hang on a minute. She was threatening to have me arrested not an hour ago.

"Well, I . . . I . . ." he stammered.

Jane held a hand to her chest and laughed. "Oh, you should have seen your face when I mentioned a baby. Bloody priceless."

Thank God. Little minx.

"You are enjoying my discomfort, aren't you?" he replied.

She ceased her mirth and met his gaze. "Only a little. But you might want to think about some of what I have said. There is a saying in the east: 'for every glance behind us, we have to look twice to the future.' It means, stop living your old life and start seeing what could be in front of you."

"You mean give up the trade?"

"I hardly think stealing and lying is a craft. And if it is, it isn't one to be proud of," she said.

Jane wasn't only whip smart. She had his measure.

If she can read me this well, I wonder when she began to see through me. Or did she have me figured out all along?

He pushed the notion firmly away, stuffing it into a dark corner of his mind, along with many of his other unpleasant moments of self-reflection. George Hawkins might well appreciate the beauty in art and jewels, but he hated the ugly man who lurked within him.

His gaze settled on the small window which overlooked the garden. The window was like most other things in the house—old and covered in grime.

"Why do you want to buy this place? I am sure if you gave a little smile or two more to your friend at the shop, he would rent it to you. If not, then wave a few coins under his hook-like nose."

He didn't like the man, but if they were going to have to do business with him, George would need to find a way to keep his temper in check.

Jane reached into her satchel and withdrew a book. After setting it onto the nearby kitchen table, she opened it where a bookmark had been placed, and held her finger to a line on the right-hand page. "Armory V. Delamirie. Court of King's Bench, 1722," she announced.

George raised an eyebrow. He was the son of a judge, and she was going to quote legal precedent at him? While he may not have managed to become a lawyer, he had studied enough of it at university to know the case. "The famous ruling regarding possession and ownership. Wasn't that the case where the chimney sweep found a ring and when he took it to a jeweler to be valued, one of the jeweler's employees tried to steal the stones?"

She nodded. "One and the same. But the main thing about the case is the idea of claiming ownership. And finders keepers. If we do find the treasure, the last thing we need is someone trying to take it away from us."

"Us?" Hope had the words rushing from George's lips before he could stop them. The mere thought of her still considering them to be partners of some sort, had him blinking hard.

I am so unworthy of this woman.

Jane nodded. "Yes, us. I think I have made my position clear when it comes to the repercussions of you betraying me. I don't think you are a dull-witted man, George, so I know you wouldn't attempt to do it a second time. I want any potential issues of legality settled before we start searching."

Jane had clearly done her homework. George's already highly held opinion of her lifted yet again. "So, what you are saying is that if we own the house, then we would have a better claim to Jane Whorwood's treasure if we happened to find it. But finders keepers rules would still apply, would they not?"

A sense of relief settled when she nodded. "I think so. Lord Harry has been doing some quiet investigating of the legalities involved in making such a claim. The legal opinions he got seem to back our case. If Jane Whorwood hid the treasure here with the intention of coming back and retrieving it, then yes, we would have solid legal grounds to keep what we find."

"Harry? Why have you involved him?"

She closed the book and sighed. "Because you don't have the money to buy the house. Whereas he and Alice do. During those first few days when you were pumped full of laudanum and recovering from the surgery on your shoulder, the three of us met and came up with a plan. They will lend you the money, and you will buy the house. In turn, I will rent it from you, so that I can establish legal rights."

"You could, of course, just have me arrested once you find the treasure," he replied.

Jane raised an eyebrow. "Yes. That thought has crossed my mind more than once. You should endeavor to remember that, just in case you are ever tempted to do me wrong again."

George had the sudden uncomfortable feeling that he was arriving partway through the second act of a play, one where he was going to have to pay close attention in order to catch up with the story and successfully take on his appointed role.

The idea of buying the house, even if it was with Harry's money, made clear sense. "How much does the shopkeeper want for this place?"

"Two hundred pounds."

His mouth dropped open. "What? Two hundred pounds. You must be in jest. This place isn't worth one hundred. I'd give you twenty for it and expect change. The man is a thief."

She gave him a pot-calling-the-kettle-black look, and George did his best to bite his tongue.

"I know it is a stupid amount of money, but this is an up-and-coming area," she replied.

"Up-and-coming what? Have hovels suddenly become fashionable and I hadn't realized? I know London can be eye-wateringly expensive, but that is outrageous," he scoffed.

Jane crossed the floor and put a hand on his arm. Her touch, though light, had an immediate calming effect on George. He glanced at her fingers; no woman had ever affected him in such a way.

It took the last vestiges of his self-control to stop himself from leaning in and simply kissing her. He was still in two minds as to whether he should when Jane took a step back, and the moment was broken.

What would she have done if I had tried to kiss her? Would she have stopped me?

Jane cleared her throat. "Did you know that during the civil war, almost all of the crown jewels were either sold or melted down?"

Most people knew that the current royal jewels were only of recent origin. That much of the previous splendor of former English kings and queens was now lost to history. Under the military dictatorship of the puritan Oliver Cromwell, many fine things had been destroyed. "Yes, but what has the crown jewels got to do with us?"

A soft, knowing smile now sat on Jane's lips. A smile which held a thousand promises.

She knows something. Of course, she does.

"Some of the items which were destined to be sold never made it into Cromwell's hands. Charles is rumored to have given many valuable pieces to Jane Whorwood in the hope that she could sell them and use the proceeds to help restore him to the throne. From what I have been able to discover, she didn't manage to get rid of the last of those jewels before she was finally made to return to her violent and abusive husband. He kept her locked up for some time, after which she never returned to London." Jane reached into the satchel and took out a bundle of letters, brandishing them at George.

"What are they?"

"These are facsimiles of the letters which Jane sent to a female friend in London over the years, asking her to check on the house. I found the originals in the museum a few months ago and made my own copies. Right to the end, she intended to come back here and retrieve the treasure but failing health and old age finally caught up with her."

The rundown, dingy house suddenly transformed before George's eyes. Where only a few minutes ago he had seen nothing but filth and decay, he now saw opportunity. George's gaze flittered around the room, his experienced criminal mind coming up with all manner of places where loot could have been hidden. He itched to tug at loose boards and rap on walls.

Jane chuckled. "I see I might have changed your opinion about this place."

How many people have lived in this house in the last hundred or so years?

Someone could have discovered the treasure long ago and quietly disposed of it. This could all be a wild goose chase. But what if it wasn't?

"How do you know the jewels or whatever Charles gave Jane still exists? They too might have been melted down and disappeared during the intervening years," he replied.

She pointed to the floor. Dust already caked the hem of Jane's skirts simply from her having walked across the room. She gestured to the walls. George peered at them, trying to decipher their original color.

I am sure they were not painted a moldy black.

"Look how dirty it is in here. No one has lived in this house for many, many years. I have it on good authority that it was used to store coal for a long time, only recently being cleared because the landlord wants to sell. They call this place Coal Yard Lane for good reason."

George's mouth turned dry at the mere possibility that they could be standing close to hidden treasure. Treasure that he and Jane could legally claim and then change into honest money.

This is the opportunity you have been looking for.

She was trusting him. After all that he had done, Jane was still prepared to give him another chance. It left him humbled and shamed.

I don't deserve this.

"Why are you putting your faith in my hands? I have already betrayed you once. What is to say I won't do it again?" he asked.

Jane shrugged. "Because you and I are not so different. We

are both people seeking a way to a different life. To a better one. And, if I were honest, I still feel a little guilty over having shot you."

George had already identified several weak spots in Jane's plan, ones which he could exploit in order to double-cross her if he so chose. He had done the dirty on enough people in his life to know it would be easy for him to do it again.

But you won't, because this is different.

Jane was offering more than just the means for George to secure possible future wealth. She was giving him the chance to finally turn his back on his lawless ways. To become a better man.

"You still haven't explained why you could possibly think me not capable of committing another act of treachery against you," he said.

Jane reached into her coat pocket and produced a pistol, which she then pointed at George. A chill of fear slid down his back. The last time he had seen that weapon, it had been fired at him.

He blinked slowly when Jane cocked the gun, the click of the hammer echoing in the still of the room.

"I believe I can trust you, George Hawkins, because the next time you even think of betraying me, I will use this on you. And when I do, the best surgeon in all of England will not be able to save you."

Bloody hell. I think I might have just fallen in love.

Chapter Seventeen

She was taking a huge risk in trusting George. But without him and his friends, Jane would never have the money to buy the house and search properly for the treasure. She certainly didn't want the dodgy owner of the property as her landlord. He would be the sort to think he had the right to drop by for a friendly *chat* whenever the mood so took him.

Point made, she put the pistol back into her pocket.

Perhaps now is a good time to set a few more ground rules.

"Harry said you were tired of living the life of a thief. That you wanted a way to forge a new future. While I commend your change of heart, I don't think attempting to steal Baldwin's crown was the right way to go about things." She wasn't sure if she would ever stop being angry with him over that ridiculous and dangerous stunt.

The look of embarrassed shame which sat on George's face gave her a glimmer of hope.

"I'm going to say this every day until I am convinced that you believe me. I am sorry, Jane. I am sorry I betrayed you. I am sorry I hurt you. And I am going to do everything in my power to gain your forgiveness."

Jane gave the merest of nods to George's words. The pain

of what he had done to her was still too raw. Her heart was a long way from forgiving, let alone healing.

You would have thought I'd have learned from the last blackguard in my life. Obviously not.

"Let's set aside your guilt and consider what is to be done. Here is my plan. Harry will prepare a bank instruction for the purchase of the house. Then you and I will sign a suitable tenancy agreement. I shall move in here and begin the process of looking for the treasure," she said.

George shook his head. "I don't like that last part."

"You don't trust me? Are you serious?"

He drew closer, and she caught a hint of his manly scent. While he had been staying with Harry and Alice, George had obviously not had the use of his personal cologne. Rising above the notes of fresh soap was a natural essence that was purely him.

A shiver of need thrilled through her body.

Why did I have to fall for such a rogue? There must be a nice gentleman who I could fall in love with, someone who is reliable. A little voice in the back of her mind chuckled and whispered. *You don't like safe men. A predictable man would bore you stupid.*

George cleared his throat. "I didn't say I did not trust you. What I meant was that you won't be staying in this house all on your own. I will be here with you."

As she opened her mouth to protest, he held up his hand.

"I am assuming that in the time since you have been back in London that you haven't lived in this part of the city. The jest about it being an up-and-coming area was just that. This is a dangerous place, especially at night. I am not having you sleeping here all by yourself. Especially knowing the type of neighbors you'll have. If you are going to move into my house, then so shall I."

Oh no.

He drew closer still, coming to stand so that he towered over her. But if his intention was to have her cower to his physical presence, Jane was ready to set George's mind to right. Placing a hand against his chest, she pushed back.

It should have been enough, but he remained firmly rooted to the spot. He took hold of her hand and lifted it to his lips, placing soft kisses in the middle of her palm—kisses that sent heat racing to her most secret of places.

If only you didn't have such an effect over me.

"If we are going to be partners in this endeavor, then we must work together. I won't have you placed at risk of harm. Don't fight me on this, because you won't win." His other hand lazily traced its way up and down her arm. The soft smile on his face informed Jane that he knew exactly what this was doing to her.

"Let go of me, George," she said.

He leaned in, and their foreheads touched.

"But I haven't finished apologizing yet."

His lips came down on hers, and all thoughts of pushing him away fled her mind.

Their other kisses had been slow and delicious, fueled by a glass or two of wine at the end of a pleasant evening by the river. This embrace was something entirely different. It was filled with heat and a passion that spoke of more than just joining forces to find the secret treasure, of them being bound to one another while traveling the road ahead.

Warm, strong fingers speared into her hair and gripped tight, setting her senses alight. There was something about a man holding a woman in such a way that had always thrilled Jane. It was a silent declaration of possession that she yearned for.

His tongue swept into her mouth, and she groaned. She exalted as he claimed all that she offered: every touch, every silent promise of forgiveness.

Yes.

For the longest time, George held her, his lips working masterfully over hers. It was only when he finally broke the embrace that she glanced down and caught sight of both her hands firmly gripping the front of his coat.

"If I was a more honorable man, I would say that we had just sealed our deal with a kiss, but since we both know that is not the case, we should get things in writing," he said.

Jane released her hold. She sucked in a deep breath, but it did little to calm her racing heart. "Yes. I have an agreement in my satchel. Harry and Alice insisted that I have it drawn up, and I was most grateful that they did. After all I have been through in the past few years, it would be the ultimate irony to lose the treasure because I foolishly let my heart rule my head."

Chapter Eighteen

The deed of sale for the house was signed and sealed within a week, the rental agreement finalized a few minutes later. George Hawkins was now the proud owner of his own dilapidated hovel, and Jane Scott his new tenant.

He also owed Lord Harry Steele the princely sum of two hundred pounds. Harry had offered to buy the house himself, but George and Jane were adamant that whatever treasure they might discover should be theirs alone. They didn't want anyone else having a legal claim over the property.

With the instruction letter from George's banker held tightly in his grubby hand, the former owner of number 11 Coal Yard Lane handed over the keys.

"Of course, when you open for business, you will oblige me with a few free visits to your girls." He leaned in close, sharing his unwashed aroma with George. "But I would settle for an hour with that Jane girl. I reckon she would be a right goer on her back that one."

George crushed the keys between his fingers, ignoring the pain of the iron as it dug into his flesh. He would love nothing more than to punch the man square in the face with them. The only thing holding him back was the reluctance to create an enemy of his neighbor.

He took several steps away from the man and glanced up at the front of the house. "Yes, well, we plan to do some renovations on the place before hanging out the sign for business. It needs a bit of work. Can't have clients complaining about the filth," he replied.

The man frowned. A quizzical look sat on his face.

Yes, I expect you are the sort of chap who has one bath a year whether you need it or not.

George had conducted some quiet investigations into the man's background, and they shared a number of mutual criminal acquaintances. It wouldn't do his cause any favors to go throwing punches. Personal vendettas were never good for business, especially when some of those associates were people George and Jane would likely need in order to sell some of the treasure when the time came.

If the time comes.

As the shopkeeper headed back to his store, George made his way to the front door of his new home. He sighed as he stepped inside. "Bloody hell, I have gone seriously into debt for this pile of shit. There had better be a bag of gold coins hidden somewhere or I will never get out from under my money problems."

Harry would never force the issue of repayment—he didn't need the money—but Jane was another matter. If they could find the treasure, George might stand a chance of keeping Jane in his life. Permanently.

While he waited for Jane to arrive, George took the opportunity to familiarize himself with the layout of the house.

There were four main floors, including three upper ones. A tiny cellar which had a good six inches of foul-smelling water covering its floor sat under a wooden cover in the corner of the kitchen. George prayed they found the treasure before anyone had to venture into that disgusting hole.

I don't think we will be preparing any meals in this kitchen.

Outside at the rear of the house was a small yard. It had a long-forgotten vegetable patch, a privy of unknown age, and what looked like an old oak tree.

As he stood looking at the tree, George imagined sitting under it on a warm summer's day. Jane would be resting her head in his lap while she told him another fascinating story of her life in the east. He would pass her a glass of wine and she would sip from it before offering her lips for yet another of his gentle kisses.

Now that would be a perfect day.

"Why did I try to steal the crown?" he muttered.

She might well have agreed to go into this venture with him, even permitted his tender regard, but would Jane ever truly trust him again?

"There you are."

He snapped out of his daydream and turned as Jane appeared out of the back of the house. As she approached him across the pale brown dirt which covered most of the yard, a thought struck him.

I was certain I had secured the front door.

"How did you manage to get in?" he asked.

She rolled her eyes. "You Europeans might think you invented everything, but a great many of the world's innovations were actually born in other places. I have my own set of skeleton keys—so I picked the lock."

George couldn't stop himself from grinning. This woman was a marvel, his equal in so many ways. The mere thought of her being able to break into the house had his manhood giving its own twitch of appreciation.

Calm down. There is plenty of work to be done. Save your lust for later.

"I was just giving the place a bit of a look over. It certainly seems that no one has lived here for quite some time," he said.

Jane came and stood at his side. "The state of the house is favorable for our venture, but not so good for us actually living here. I've examined upstairs, and there are two bedrooms which we could use if we so chose, but at the moment I would rather leave them empty. Spaces kept clear are easier to search. The downstairs parlor is clean enough for us to use. We can set up camp in there. Alice kindly gave me some blankets and pillows, so our sleeping arrangements should be set. If the rest of our efforts prove fruitless, we will search that room last."

George silently chided himself. He hadn't got to the practicalities of their situation. Rather, his focus had been on the house and where Jane Whorwood might have stashed the jewels.

The most he had managed to achieve before coming here this morning was to visit his parents and explain that he was going to take up residency at the RR Coaching Company offices for a time in order to help Stephen with Toby. His mother had given him a most quizzical look at the mention of him minding a small child, but instead of saying anything about it, she had immediately summoned a footman to retrieve George's travel bag.

He had muffled a wince when her tight hug pressed on his wounded shoulder. For once he had made his mother happy. It was a rare thing.

George could, of course, understand her reaction; it was most out of character for him to actually take responsibility for someone other than himself. His mother had been begging him for several years to grow up and find a good woman to share his life. He dreaded to think how many more names Mrs. Hawkins had added to the list of candidates for the role of future-wife of her errant son during his absence.

He glanced at Jane. As far as he was concerned, his mother could stop adding names.

Don't waste your time, Mama. I think I might have already found the right one.

Convincing Jane of that life-altering fact might, however, be a different story.

Chapter Nineteen

❦

It took the better part of the rest of the day to make the small kitchen and front parlor room clean and habitable for the two of them. A great deal of scrubbing was required to remove the thick coating of greasy dust which seemed to cover every surface. The fireplace in the kitchen was old and broken, the chimney blocked with years of soot and grime.

"I don't think we will be doing much cooking in there," said Jane, stepping into the parlor.

George nodded. "I dread to think what has crawled into this place over the years and died. If we want a hot supper, there are plenty of taverns around here that serve decent food. The rest we can get from the local markets. Worst case, we pay Harry and Alice a visit in the evenings."

She frowned at him. "I think Harry and Alice have already done more than they should for this little project. Which reminds me, they said you were not going to tell any of the other members of the RR Coaching Company about all this. Can I ask why? I understand why you would want to keep things secret, but not trusting all of your closest friends seems a little odd."

George swept the last patch of dirt on the floor into a

pile, then rested his broom against the wall. If he was going to win her trust, he would have to let Jane in on a few secrets. "The rogues of the road, as we like to refer to ourselves, have always operated on a need-to-know basis. From what I understand, Stephen and Gus are both involved in a matter of great importance at the moment. They are helping an old friend of ours from Spain who is trying to locate a missing noblewoman. They have enough to deal with."

"And what about the Duke of Monsale? I would have thought since he is your leader you would tell him."

George paused for a moment.

Monsale, now there is a whole other sordid story. You think my life is complicated—you have no idea what that man has lived through.

"Monsale might be our notional leader, but I can't say he is someone whom you would blindly place your trust in. While he is rich, he is also a man who gets a thrill out of screwing the very last penny out of a situation. If he knew about the treasure, he would find a way to cheat us out of it."

"But I thought he was your friend," she replied.

George nodded. "He is, but Monsale has limited capacity when it comes to loyalty."

"What do mean?"

"Andrew McNeal, as he was known until only a few years ago, grew up on an island in the North Atlantic. His father worked out of Bermuda with the infamous Hezekiah Frith. They were pirates, blood thirsty and cruel."

He didn't want to go any further into the sordid history of the Monsale family. If Jane remained in George's life, she would find out the rest soon enough. "Besides, he is back in the country at his estate, overseeing the planting of his crops. The Duke of Monsale hasn't got time to come to London and dig in the mud alongside us."

Jane glanced at her dirty hands. "I'm going to the water

pump at the end of the street to clean up. Then we should look to go and find some food."

Her response to his words told George all he needed to know. Jane Scott was wondering, yet again, how the devil she had got mixed up with such a bunch of crooks and thieves.

"I ask myself the same question at least once a day," he muttered.

But unlike Jane, George already knew the answer.

Because you are as wicked as the rest of them.

※

A couple of bottles of ale and a beef pie was the regal supper which sat before them later that night. Jane licked her fingers. "The meat sauce was delicious. We should put that pie shop on our list of regular dining places."

George, who was still chewing the last of his pie, nodded his agreement.

Picking up her empty bottle, Jane got to her feet. With hands on hips, she surveyed the parlor. It was a small room, much like all the other spaces in the house. She couldn't recall having ever lived in such a cramped place. "I think we should put the blankets and pillows down in the corner and that will mean we are as far away from the draft which comes under the door as is possible."

George turned his head in the direction of where she'd nodded. The look on his face changed from happily satisfied to that of surprised disappointment. "You mean for us to sleep on the floor?"

"We don't really have an option. I haven't yet discovered a mattress in the house, and even if there was, I doubt we would wish to sleep on it." She snorted as George's unhappy expression turned pitiful. Sleeping on the floor had been something she had done most of her life. At the height of a Byblos summer, the whole Scott family would take their mats up to the flat roof of their house and enjoy a good night's sleep in the cool air. The lack of a bed hadn't posed an issue for her, but it clearly did for George.

Poor thing. Fancy never having to rough it.

"Let's see how we go tonight. If you find it too uncomfortable, then perhaps you will need to look at getting a mattress which you can store out of the way during the day," she said.

George downed his remaining ale and got to his feet. He winced as he placed a hand in the small of his back. "Even sitting on the floor for an hour hurts my hips and knees. I shall try this sleeping arrangement one night, but something already tells me that first thing tomorrow I will scraping up whatever coins I have and purchasing a well-stuffed mattress."

Jane moved closer and came to stand behind him, placing her hands on his hips. "If you slowly shift your weight from right to left and back again, you should be able to loosen up those hips with gentle stretches."

He glanced at her from over his shoulder. His eyebrows raised in obvious doubt at her advice.

"Wait until I teach you how to roll your hips like a proper belly dancer before you give me any more of your disapproving stares, George Hawkins," she teased.

"Belly dancing? What on earth does that involve?"

She turned him to face her, then took a step back. With hands held out at her side, she began to trace a slow figure eight with her hips. Her skirts lifted and fell in time with her movements. "This is the dance of the east, though usually the woman is dressed in traditional attire and you can actually see her stomach, hence its name."

Their gazes met. There was the unmistakable haze of lust in George's eyes. She dropped her arms and stopped dancing.

"Well, something like that. It has been a long time since I saw it danced in the town of Byblos."

He reached out and slipped his hand around her waist,

drawing her to him. "I doubt I shall get much sleep tonight, so will you tell me a little more of your life. Of your family?"

She closed her eyes as tears threatened. "You don't really want to know my past, do you?"

Warm, soft kisses traced their way along her neck.

Oh, George, you are such a rogue. And I am weak when it comes to you.

"If you and I are to work together, to truly trust each other, I need to know everything," he murmured.

Where do I begin?

She lifted her face and stared into his gentle brown eyes. She wanted nothing more than to believe in this man. To have him take her in his arms and kiss her senseless. If they were locked in a sensual embrace, then maybe, just maybe, she wouldn't have to share her painful past with him.

George brushed a soft kiss on her lips, then drew back. He kept his arm around her. "Tell me about your family."

Chapter Twenty

Jane's whole body stiffened. Her gaze fell to the floor.

"You only have to say just as much as you are comfortable with telling me. Nothing more," he said.

She sighed. "People think the Mediterranean Sea is a calm place, but it's not. Just over three years ago, my family and I left the Ottoman Empire. We sailed from Constantinople, with the intention of stopping over in Sicily for a time so that we could visit the ancient Phoenician temples and settlements on the western side of the island."

He waited patiently as Jane paused, releasing his hold on her just a little. Enough to let her know that if she wanted to create a physical distance between them, he wouldn't stop her. "Go on," he gently urged.

"We sailed over thirteen hundred miles, and, in the end, Sicily wasn't that far away. We almost made it—" Her voice cut off as she pulled free of George's embrace. Instinctively, he took a step toward her, but she held out her hand. "Don't. Please. Just give me a minute. I haven't told anyone this story, so you have to forgive me if I struggle."

"Jane." The weight of pain in his heart at seeing her in such distress was almost too much for George to bear. He had founded his whole existence, his life on lies. Experiencing such honest emotion from another person was profoundly confronting.

"A storm blew up. The waves were so high, they simply crashed over the ship. It was an endless onslaught. We stayed in our cabin and prayed. When the captain came and told us that the boat was in danger of foundering, I knew we were in serious trouble." She took another long, deep breath. "Within an hour, we had hit a reef off the north-east coast of Malta, and the ship sank. The last time I saw my family was when we were all assembled on the deck, just before one last terrible wave hit us."

"Did anyone else make it to shore?" he asked.

Jane shook her head. "No." She made stiff, unhurried steps toward the door. George was in two minds as to what he should do, but he let her go.

A few minutes later, he found Jane standing outside in the garden, staring up at the grey, smokey London night sky. His boots crunched on the dry, hard ground as he approached, and she turned.

"It's strange to live in a city where the stars cannot be easily seen. You get the odd glimpse of them, but nothing like what you experience in the east," she said.

George came and took a spot beside her. "I cannot imagine what it must be like to lose your whole family and find yourself alone in the world. But I promise that you won't ever be on your own again."

The weight of his words was that of a vow. George held out his hand, and Jane slipped her fingers into his. They were in this together, and he wouldn't ever let her go.

Chapter Twenty-One

A nice thick mattress arrived midmorning the following day. When Jane had woken just after dawn, it was to the sight of a sleeping George slumped against the parlor room wall, his head dropped against his chest. It looked terribly uncomfortable, and his complaints about a stiff neck and back soon confirmed her suspicions.

The fact that George had purchased only one mattress, albeit a large one, did not go unnoticed.

I wonder if he has plans to share it. It would be presumptuous of him if does, but then again, I wouldn't complain.

She helped him to drag it into the parlor, where George leaned it against the wall.

"Hopefully a better night's sleep tonight," he said.

"I am sure you will be comfy," she replied.

There was a moment of awkward silence, after which George cleared his throat. "So, are we going to put a strategy together as to how the house should be searched? I mean, we need to make sure we work methodically so as to ensure that we don't overlook anywhere."

"While you were out indulging yourself in a nice piece of padded luxury, I started on something. Come and have a look." She led him into the kitchen where she had earlier spread out a large piece of paper on the table. Jane pointed to the rough plan she had made of each floor of the house and also the rear garden. "I have noted where various cupboards and fireplaces are situated, as well as the number of floorboards in each room. I thought we could tick them off as we search; that way we won't miss anything."

He gave her mud map a slow looking over, pointing out things she had missed and offering helpful suggestions. She accepted them, grateful to have someone else's input.

"We could use chalk to mark the actual places we have looked. I find I am a visual person, and if I can walk into a room and see where we have explored, it will help me enormously," said George.

Jane shot him a wary glance. "Is that a skill that you've developed from casing places when you were planning to rob them? Like what you did with the embassy."

The dirty look she got in reply informed her exactly what George thought of that remark, but Jane wasn't done.

"George, you were making notes about the security of the exhibition the night we first met. You can't possibly be sensitive and precious about your past."

I really do hope you are going to put your criminal life in the past. If not, then we have no chance whatsoever of a future.

"I'm not being testy about what I have done. I just find it uncomfortable to discuss such things with you." A clearly annoyed George raked his fingers through the short strands of his hair. "And yes, I can fully understand how asinine that makes me seem, but it's the truth. I want to move on from that life, and this—with you, is the best opportunity I have ever had to do just that."

A surprising sense of guilt over having called his morals into question crept up on Jane. It was foolish, because despite all his protests, George *had* been a master thief.

What would have happened if he had succeeded in stealing Baldwin's crown and tried to sell it?

She smiled slyly at the thought. One day she might just tell him. But that was not today.

"I'm sorry, George. It's hard to look at you and not see a wicked rogue. In time hopefully my view will change."

He gave one last look at the sheet of paper on the table, then turned on his heel. His voice drifted back to her from farther down the hallway. "I plan on it."

The rest of the day was spent looking in all the obvious places for the treasure trove: cupboards, behind doors, even inside the filthy mattress they discovered in the attic. By the time they were ready to use the clean water they had gotten earlier from the nearby public water pump at the end of the street, and washed the dust from themselves, Jane and George were both exhausted.

"Tomorrow, I think we should focus on the floorboards," she said.

He nodded. "Loose ones first then, room by room, the rest of them. I will go and buy some chalk first thing so we can mark our progress as we go."

If the floors yielded nothing, next would be the roof, the chimneys, and the fireplaces. Then the outside. Jane did not look forward to digging up the yard, especially not near the privy. From the crusty ground around it, she could tell that over the long years, the cesspit underneath had been left to regularly overflow. It was probably still full now. The idea of stepping on something wet in the dark on her way to the toilet made her gag.

Which reminds me, I need to pay a coin to the nightsoil man and make sure he keeps it clear while we are living here.

For all its grand reputation, London was a filthy city. The great network of aqueducts which distributed fresh water throughout Constantinople put the English capital to shame.

"I tell you what—how about I give my face and hands a

quick clean, then I will head out to buy us some supper? That will allow you a moment of privacy to have a wash," he said.

George might well be a career criminal, but he was still a gentleman. The idea of having a little time to herself held a certain appeal. George Hawkins was a man who took up a great deal of space.

And not just physically. I am always thinking of him.

"That would be lovely. Thank you, George. It's a kind and sweet gesture."

When he scowled at her words, Jane laughed.

"Oh, come now. You are not entirely a blackguard. I am beginning to suspect that underneath all your villainy you are actually a decent man."

George muttered something inaudible, but Jane caught the hint of a smile on his face. He headed out of the kitchen and toward the front door. "I won't be long. Hopefully the bakery on the corner of Brownlow Street has some apple tarts left for us."

With George gone and the house all to herself, Jane stripped off her clothes and indulged in the joy of a soap and bucket wash. As her hands worked over her naked body, she did her best not to think of him. Of how his fingers and lips would feel on her heated flesh. Of the pleasure of him filling her deeply with his manhood and bringing her to completion.

It's been far too long without a man's touch. I know he is wicked, but I want him.

The temptation to ask if George wished for her to share his soft new bed was there, but Jane worried what he would make of such a sexually forward offer. This was England, and from what she understood, women here treated the act of lovemaking as something to be ashamed of and kept purely for the marital bed.

Their connection had thus far only reached the point of kissing and hugging, though some of those kisses had been more than just tender explorations. That last one on the day they'd looked at the house had been a clear statement of claim.

Should I let him make the first move? Or is he holding back because he thinks I am inexperienced, that I am a virgin?

"Yes, well, that's not exactly the sort of thing you discuss while searching a house for lost treasure, is it? I say, George, did you happen to find the jewels? No, but I think I discovered your lost virginity." She chuckled at her own naughty jest.

But what if she could let him know that she was not some prim and proper miss? That a sexual relationship between them could be more than just a possibility?

A loud rap at the front door stirred Jane from her musings. Grabbing a towel, she quickly dried her body and slipped on the clean gown she had left hanging over the back of a chair.

"Coming, just a minute," she called.

She was still finger-combing her damp hair when she opened the door. "Did you forget your key, George . . ."

The figure at the door wasn't George. It was the lascivious and altogether creepy former owner of the house.

Bloody hell, what does he want?

"Hello, darlin'. I saw your fancy man heading off a short while ago. I was thinkin' you might be lonely and in need of company."

Jane gave him a tight smile. "That is very considerate of you, but I am fine. Good evening." She went to push the door closed, but a large, dirty boot was jammed in the space.

Her heart began to race as her gaze settled on the beady eyes which peered through the gap. George had been gone for a good fifteen minutes, and if he had only gone to the nearby tavern for food, hopefully he was on his way back.

But how long was the time between then and now? Would she be able to sweet-talk this letch into going home and leaving her alone, or would he seize the opportunity to take what was so clearly written in his eyes?

"Come now. You don't have to be all coy wiv me. I like the ones who talk in a posh voice; it gets me cock hard. But the truth is, you just have to get on your back and let me do it," he said.

George, where are you?

"I think you may have the wrong end of the stick. I am not on the game, and he is not my pimp. What we said before we bought the house was just in jest; you must have realized, that? My husband and I are going to clean up the house and live here. He says this area is ripe for new development," she replied, swallowing a lump of fear. She pushed against the door, hoping that he might take the hint.

He didn't. Instead, he forced his way farther into the gap.

"I am sorry. I didn't know we were having company this evening."

Jane could have wept with relief at the sound of George's voice.

The shopkeeper hastily retreated out of the doorway as George muscled his way past him and into the house. He stopped and gave Jane a tender kiss on the lips. "Sorry I took so long, sweetheart."

She accepted the bag of food from his hands and moved toward the kitchen. From over her shoulder came a hurried "Good night" from their neighbor, followed by the reassuring sound of the door being firmly closed and locked.

Jane had just set the parcel on the table when George appeared at her shoulder.

"What did he want?" he asked.

She sucked in a shuddering breath. "Me."

Strong arms wrapped around her, and a warm kiss was pressed to her forehead. As George stroked his hand over her hair, Jane quietly counted her blessings. He might well be a rogue, but he was also very much her hero.

Chapter Twenty-Two

"I really should go and have a firm word with him," said George.

Truthfully, a word wasn't all he wanted to give the man. If George made the short trip to the front door of their neighbor's home, he was more than likely going to kick it in. Then the disgusting creep would get a violent and bloody lesson in what George Hawkins did to the likes of men who had in mind to force themselves on a woman.

I shall meet with each one of our mutual acquaintances and make certain that they never do business with you again. I will ruin you.

"We need to keep him on side, at least until we have finished searching the house. We can't afford to make an enemy of him. With luck, he got the message tonight," she said.

"As you hopefully did too. I won't have your safety compromised. From now on, if you are alone in the house, you don't answer the bloody door. I don't care if it's the King of England on the other side."

He didn't want to think about what might have happened

tonight if he hadn't realized that the baker's shop closed early on a Monday and returned to the house.

Jane had assured him that nothing had happened, and she was fine, but anger still coursed through George's veins. It was only her insistence on them eating their supper and discussing the details of the treasure hunt for the following day that kept him from marching out the front door.

I just want to throttle that bastard. Fancy thinking, he could lay his hands on Jane.

"I promise I will not open the door without knowing who it is on the other side. To be honest, I am a more than a little disappointed in myself for having done so. You would think after all this time of being on my own that I would know better. And I do," she replied.

George set his mug of ale on the table. They really had to do something about the fireplace in the kitchen. He would kill for a hot cup of tea or even a lukewarm coffee.

But right now, all I want is to kill someone.

"I thought it was clever of you to tell him I was your husband. Perhaps we should keep that story going. Maybe if he understands that you are not available for any sexual services, he might get the hint," said George.

"Agreed. If he thinks I am not a whore, then he might back off. He didn't dally for one second the moment you appeared. He knows you are on to him, so I doubt he would be foolish enough to try again," she said.

He sighed. Jane was being far too cool about all this; and that had George worried.

Does she even realize what he could have done to her?

It was time to have a difficult, but necessary conversation.

"Did your mother ever give you *the talk*? I mean, about what happens between a man and a woman. Kissing is one thing, but sexual congress is another matter entirely," he said.

A shy smile appeared on her lips.

Is that a blush? Oh. I should have put it more delicately than that. I am a dolt.

Jane reached across the table and after taking hold of one of his hands, gave it a reassuring pat. "No, my mother didn't ever get around to giving me the full story about sex. But she explained enough for me to have figured it out before my first time," she replied.

Their gazes met. Jane was not a virgin. *Hmm.*

"So, you are telling me you are not an innocent? I mean, not that it matters. I just . . ."

Jane rose and leaned over the table before placing a soft, inviting kiss on George's lips. She beckoned for him to come closer, and when he did, she whispered into his ear, "From personal experience, I am well aware of what happens when a man and a woman lay together. If you wish it so, I could share your mattress and show you what I have learned."

Wish it so? Heavens, it was all he thought of every time she was near. In his mind, George had developed quite a detailed image of what Jane would look like naked. The prospect of seeing it for real, in the flesh, had him licking his lips.

She got to her feet and came to stand behind him where he sat at the table. Her warm fingers settled on the back of his neck and began to gently rub. "You need to relax. Your neck is all stiff."

Her hands moved lower, and George groaned as she dug into the tightly knotted muscles in his shoulders. One night of sleeping sitting upright had made a mess of him. "I've slept on the deck of Gus's yacht many a time and not woken up like this; I must be getting old."

"Gus? He's one of the rogues of the road I haven't met. Would I like him?"

A spark of hot jealousy pierced George's heart. Gus was a lady's man through and through. If he got anywhere near Jane, there was every chance he would turn on the charm and have her fainting away in his arms. "Gus keeps pretty much to himself. He is busy with the boat. Someday, I expect you and he will meet."

Jane's fingers stilled, and she whispered in his ear, "What you are really saying is that he is devilishly handsome, and females swoon before him."

Blast Gus and his good looks.

Not that George was in any sort of position to claim ownership of Jane; especially not after all he'd done. The prospect of her falling under the spell of Gus had him grinding his teeth.

She chuckled wickedly. "Alice told me all about Augustus Trajan Jones. Let me reassure you that when it comes to him, you have nothing to fear."

George cleared his throat. "Well, I wasn't concerned—if that's what you are thinking."

Under the table, his cock twitched, growing a little hard. He could have sworn it had its own voice and was demanding that he do something about the situation and soon.

Her fingers went back to untangling the tension in his muscles. "Close your eyes and let me work on you."

George did as he was told. The sensation of blood working its way freely back into his muscles was a welcome relief. "Is this masterful manipulation of my body another of the wonders of the east?"

A soft, warm kiss was placed on the side of his cheek. And then another. By the time Jane's lips touched his neck, George was already semi-hard. His self-restraint was ready to snap.

"I think you had better stop that now. If you don't, I am going to have a long and uncomfortable night ahead of me. I won't get any sleep."

When Jane nipped her teeth on the bottom of George's earlobe, the battle was over. His last line of defense shattered.

He rose from the chair, scooped her up in his arms, and

headed for the parlor. "I think it's time we broke that new mattress in—what do you say?"

Jane squealed with delight. "I thought you'd never ask!"

Chapter Twenty-Three

George swore as they entered the parlor. The mattress was still propped up against the wall, their bed not made. He set Jane on her feet. "Stay there."

He was all manly man in his rough way of speaking to her, and she loved it. She could only hope he was just as demanding of her body.

As George set about getting the mattress ready, Jane flicked open the top button of her gown. He growled. "Don't you dare touch another button or hook."

George's barbarian antics of carrying her had already heated Jane's blood; his words just added fuel to the fire.

After setting the mattress on the floor and tossing the blankets at one end, George closed the distance between them. Jane lifted her gaze and met his as George towered seductively over her. His whole presence oozed lust and barely controlled desire.

"George?"

"Yes."

"Strip me naked and take your pleasure." Her declaration was meant to match his, to show that she was no wilting flower he should treat with virginal reverence. She wanted

George, and all that he could give. Yet when his fingers touched her cheek, it was with a tenderness and care that made Jane shiver.

"I've never been with a woman just to sate my own needs. It has always been with the clear understanding of mutual satisfaction. I want to be more than that with you, to create a real connection."

Her heart gave a little skip.

"If you are willing, I would have us become lovers," he added.

"Yes."

A warm, tender kiss sealed their agreement.

George loosened the rest of Jane's buttons, then lifted her gown over her head and dropped it to the floor. As he worked the laces of her stays free, he stopped every so often to place a soft, light kiss in the crook of her neck. Jane closed her eyes and sighed. This was heaven.

It seemed an eternity since she had last felt like a woman, been treated as such. Not Miss Scott the governess or J. Scott the antiquities expert—just Jane. A flesh-and-blood woman wanted by a man purely for being just her.

He nipped his teeth against the side of her neck and Jane's core pulsed. The small sting of pain stirred her desires from their slumber. "George," she murmured.

He pulled back and met her gaze. "Tell me if you don't want me touching you that way. I want to know all that you do and don't like."

She reached for the placket of his trousers, giving him a sultry smile as the top fastening came free. "I would rather we show one another."

As the second button loosened, his hardened cock sprang forward against the fabric. Jane brushed the front of his falls aside and took George firmly in hand, giving a hard squeeze. His groan was all the encouragement she needed.

Long strokes of his member had him placing his hand on

her shoulder and his breath coming in short rasps. It was wonderful to have this sort of power over a man once more, to know she had him captive.

"Jane. You will be the death of me if you keep that up," he murmured.

He stole her lips with a long, deep kiss. Tongues tangled together as they bit and kissed each other's mouths with ever-increasing urgency.

When he took a hold of her wrist and ceased her strokes, George panted, "I want you. I need you. We have to be rid of our clothes."

In under a minute the rest of their garments had joined Jane's gown on the floor.

Naked, she lay on the mattress, welcoming George with open arms as he kicked the last of his boots off and joined her.

They picked up where they had left off with deep, passionate kisses. Jane spread her thighs wide to accommodate George as he settled between her legs.

He broke the kiss, only to then blaze a trail of scorching nips and bites down her neck and all the way to one nipple. Her back arched off the mattress as George sucked the peaked bud into his mouth and drew hard on it.

"Oh!" she moaned, her fingers spearing into his hair.

If he was anything like she thought he might be, George would want to take this first time slow. But burning need had already built to fever pitch within her. The last thing she wanted was slow and easy.

"Take me now. I need you inside me. Please, George," she begged.

He rose over her and looked into her eyes. Dark pools of desire stared back at her, but above them sat a worried expression on his brow. "Don't you want me to . . ."

"No. Not this time. Maybe later."

As he set the broad head of his cock to her entrance, Jane almost wept with relief.

So long. So bloody long.

She clenched her fingers to the sides of his hips as he slowly pressed in. He withdrew for a moment, then pushed deep, seating himself fully within her.

"George!"

With his every stroke she began the familiar climb to climax, urging him on with her fingers as she dug them into his flesh.

Drawing her leg over his hip, she opened her sex more fully to him, and George began to thrust hard and fast into her. The room was soon filled with the sounds of skin on skin and Jane's cries of pleasure.

She crashed through into a blinding orgasm, her whole body feeling like it had turned to heated mercury. There were a few more frenzied strokes before George let out a loud groan and collapsed on top of her.

For a short time, they simply lay in silence in the dark, their bodies still melded together. When George eventually rolled off and flopped onto the mattress beside her, Jane retrieved a blanket from the end of the bed and threw it over them. George lay on his back, wrapping a strong arm around Jane as she snuggled against him and rested her head on his chest.

Listening to the steady, slow beat of his heart, Jane resisted the temptation to make pillow talk. She wanted to preserve this moment, to savor the memory of her and George's first time together. With luck, it wouldn't be the last.

Chapter Twenty-Four

They had made love twice the previous night. Yet from the way Jane was behaving, it was almost as if it had never happened. While George was a man used to sexual liaisons with little to no strings attached, he found her demeanor the following morning oddly unsettling. He was the one with the greatest amount of sexual experience, but the fact that Jane had any sort of romantic past did not sit easily with him.

Jealousy was a strange, new emotion to him. He could privately admit to not enjoying it in the least. Who was the man who had taken her innocence, who had also at some point held her love?

And how can I remove the memory of him from her heart?

She was his, and he would be damned if someone from her past would have any place in her memories. Not even a dark out-of-the-way corner.

It didn't matter to him. Whatever it would take, George was determined to wipe away every last trace of another man from his woman's life. He wanted Jane's heart and soul completely for himself.

After venturing out early to buy some chalk, George returned to the house where he
spent over an hour tapping against the walls and floors of the master bedroom before his curiosity and unsettled mind finally got the better of him. With a loud huff, he went in search of Jane.

He found her in the tiny attic.

"About Malta?" he began as he stepped into the room.

Jane was in the far corner, knocking against the wall. Taking a block of the chalk, she marked a big 'X' on a nearby wooden beam before coming over to where George stood. "What about Malta?"

This could be awkward.

How did a gentleman enquire as to his partner's previous sexual encounters? The fact that she was experienced should have been enough. In one respect he was grateful that she was. It meant he hadn't had to deal with the delicate matter of taking her virginity. He had heard enough rumors of wedding nights and timid brides to know he wasn't keen on deflowering any woman. But the fact that Jane had had a previous lover was a double-edged sword.

I should have been her first . . . and only.

She shook her head. "You don't want to know about Malta. You want to know who *he* was, and why the devil we didn't end up as man and wife."

"Yes."

🙢

She wasn't surprised that George had come seeking answers. Those sorts of things were important to many men. And George Hawkins was definitely the possessive, dare she say jealous type.

"Come on downstairs and we can have some of the leftover bread from breakfast as our elevenses. There should be some clean water in the bucket for a tepid cup of tea," she said.

He followed her out of the attic and down the creaky stairs to the kitchen. If she was going to have to relive some of the most painful moments of her life, Jane was certainly not going to do it on an empty stomach.

She took up her usual spot at the kitchen table and George sat in the chair opposite. It was funny how quickly they had settled into the routine of playing at being an old married couple.

"Well, you know our ship ran aground just off the coast of Malta and I was the only member of my family to survive. What I haven't told you was what my life was like in the intervening years between then and my return to England," she said.

George shuffled about in his seat. "Before you go on, I need you to understand why this all matters to me. I know you had a life before me, and we haven't been together very long, but I want to understand the sort of man who could possibly love a woman such as you and not be able to keep her."

Oh, the irony. If only it had been that way.

Jane closed her eyes for a moment, letting her mind wander into the hidden recesses where she had carefully tucked away the recollections of her first love. She sighed at the bitter-sweet memories. "His name was Pietro. And he was the most beautiful man I have ever met. You usually only see men such as him in paintings by the old Renaissance masters."

There was no point in trying to tell George anything but the truth. Pietro, with his long black hair and Mediterranean sun-kissed face, had been the mortal personification of an ancient Greek god. No girl in the town of Sliema had been immune to his siren's lure. Even Jane, while still in the depths of her grief, had found herself drawn to him.

George's hardened face told her all she needed to know about what he thought of Pietro. Her former Maltese lover should have been thanking his lucky stars he was some eighteen hundred miles away.

Her gaze dropped to George's tightly held fists.

I expect if you could get hold of Pietro you might do him some harm.

Not that she would stop him. Lord knew her duplicitous former lover deserved a good thrashing. "But beauty isn't everything. Especially when you have a cold heart," she added.

"What did he do?"

It was more what he didn't do that had given Jane cause for great despair, many nights of tears, and her eventual departure from Malta. "He married someone else. A local girl he barely knew, but whom he had been betrothed to since a young boy. An arrangement he hadn't seen fit to share with me. During summer last year, their families moved ahead with wedding preparations, and the first I knew about their impending marriage was when it was announced by the priest at Sunday mass. You can imagine how well I received that piece of news."

The heart-breaking agony of being tossed aside by a man she had given herself to over the course of many months had only been exacerbated by the discovery that many people had known that she and Pietro were secret lovers. Public humiliation was a sharp and unpleasant pill to swallow. The whispers and looks of pity whenever she went to the village market remained painfully in Jane's memories long after she had boarded the ship back to England.

"He sounds like a complete blackguard who didn't deserve you," replied George.

She blinked away a tear. Even now, after all this time, those words still felt hollow. Yes, Pietro was a lying bastard who had betrayed her. But she had loved him, been prepared to build a life with him on the island, to never return to England.

In the blink of an eye, her dreams of being his wife and the mother to his children had shattered to a thousand pieces, along with her heart.

"So, I packed up what was left of my pride, got on a ship, and came here." Jane rose from the table. That was as much as she wanted to share about *him* with George. Like her life in the Middle East, it was yet another door which she had closed firmly behind her.

She made it most of the way to the kitchen door, but he quickly got to his feet and intercepted her. Taking Jane by the arm, George pulled her roughly to him. "I swear by all that is holy that I would never do that to you. I will be true."

"You have to forgive me if I doubt that you have ever taken a vow and kept it, George Hawkins. But at least I know the kind of man you are. With you, there is no pretense. I don't expect you to even consider the possibility of us staying together and marrying."

She had meant it as a kindness, as a way to release him from any foolish notions of marital obligations, but the flash of dark anger which crossed his face told her he had not taken it that way. He was outraged and offended.

"So, you have no plans to ever become my wife? You would lay with me, but not take my name?" he ground out.

When she strained against his hold, George had the good sense to let her go. Jane moved closer toward the doorway. "Let's worry about finding Jane Whorwood's hidden treasure. That's all that is important at the moment. I can't deal with any other complications in my life right now."

She didn't want any grand declarations of intent from George.

If they found the cache of jewels and coins which her research had led her to believe existed, they would both be in a position to make life-altering decisions. Offers of marriage were not something one should rush into making, especially when neither party was prepared to raise or discuss the topic of love.

He knows my past. Now it's up to him to decide if he wants to be my future.

Chapter Twenty-Five

Two days later, Jane and George were sitting on the floor of the attic, silently staring at one another. There were no words for the depths of bitter disappointment which she knew he almost certainly shared with her. All they had to show for their hard work was sore muscles and bruises. Every last place they could think to look had been searched. Nothing had been found.

To top it off, they were both sporting bloodied and raw knuckles from the work of prizing the floorboards out from where they had lain for hundreds of years. George's iron crowbar, the criminal past of which Jane didn't wish to know, had come in handy for lifting the boards. Unfortunately, more than once, fingers had got in the way and been bashed as the heavy planks of wood dropped.

And while the previous three nights of lovemaking had been moments of shared ecstasy, today her heart and soul felt hollow.

Come on. Get up. You can't allow yourself to wallow. You must go on.

Those words had kept her sane over the past few years, had enabled her to survive the hardest days of grief following the loss of her family, and then Pietro. Busy hands stopped her mind from wandering into dark places.

"So, where does that leave us?" asked George.

Now, that's a question with more than one answer. Are you referring to the treasure or you and me?

And when it came to the matter of the two of them, it wasn't something Jane wished to ponder under the current circumstances. George had not taken her blanket refusal to discuss the future of their relationship all that well, but her seductive techniques whilst they lay together on the mattress each night had always won over any possible resistance he had sought to attempt.

"I checked the drawings of the house plans this morning in anticipation of the floorboards not revealing anything of value. I am going to clean out the soot and dirt from the fireplace in the kitchen. If it doesn't yield a hidden fortune, then at least we might be able to get the chimney working and have a fire. I would love to be able to boil some water here in the house," she replied.

A tired looking George simply nodded. "Alright, then I will start checking the roof. Poking a broom about might loosen something."

From the state of the fireplace in the kitchen, it appeared not to have been used for many years. There was no grate for burning wood, nor hooks to hold iron pots. For all Jane knew, the black burn marks on the bricks at the back had been there for more than a century.

Kneeling on the hard stone floor, Jane proceeded to brush away the remains of old fires. She hummed a traditional Maltese folk song as she worked but soon stopped when painful memories came rushing back. "Reckless and foolish—that was you in Malta. And you have done the same here—trusted your heart and future to a man who you don't know can be relied upon," she muttered.

Slowly, the bricks of the fireplace began to appear. Jane

scrubbed them down with a bucket and brush. Most had once been grey, the odd one or two a reddish brown. But slowly, in the right-hand rear corner of the brickwork, a new color began to appear.

These bricks were of a neater, more uniform design. It seemed that at some point in the past, repairs had been made to this part of the hearth.

"Why would you need to replace only some bricks?" she mused.

Jane stared at the chocolate-colored patch of masonry for a moment, then slowly got to her feet. "George, could you please come downstairs for a moment?" she called. Her voice was steady, but her heart raced.

He appeared in the kitchen a short time later, broom in hand. "What do you need?"

Jane pointed toward the fireplace. "Notice anything odd or unusual?"

He crossed the floor and stood in front of the brickwork. Jane patiently waited.

And waited.

When he finally turned and faced her, the hint of a grin was on his lips.

"Why aren't you more excited?" she asked.

George slipped a hand about her waist and drew Jane in close. He kissed her gently on the forehead. "One thing you learn when you are a thief is not to get your hopes up. I've lost count of the number of times in my younger years when I thought I was about to discover Eldorado only to end up with nothing."

Her shoulders dropped. It wasn't George's fault; he was obviously trying to be helpful, to temper her excitement, but it wasn't what Jane wanted to hear. She pulled out of his embrace.

"Wait a minute," he said, and walked from the kitchen.

He disappeared for a brief moment before reappearing

bearing a mallet and chisel. He knelt in front of the odd-colored section of the fireplace and set the chisel against the mortar of one of the bricks. With steady knocks, he chipped away at the edges.

Setting his tools aside, George then worked one of the bricks free. "Damn," he muttered.

"What?"

"There is another brick behind it. I was hoping there might be something else," he replied.

Jane chewed impatiently on the nail of her left thumb.

Please let there be something there.

"What about the other bricks? Could you chip around one of those and see if there is anything different?" she said.

George glanced back over his shoulder at her. He waved Jane over. "Come and help. There is nothing worse than standing by while someone else is working, especially when you have so much at stake."

Thank goodness you can see what the suspense is doing to me. You understand me better than most other people in my past have done.

When they made love, she had noticed that he possessed an almost innate appreciation of her needs and desires. This was in stark contrast to Pietro, who had taken the better part of two months to finally discover how to bring Jane to climax.

Two long months during which I foolishly convinced myself it was all my fault.

She stirred from her musings and knelt beside George.

He handed her the chisel and mallet before pointing to the brick next to the hole he had created. "Give that a crack or two and then I will try and shift it."

Thunk. Thunk. On the third strike, a large piece of mortar gave way. George leaned in and pulled it free. Jane moved the chisel farther along the brick and gave it another hard strike. More joinery came away.

George wriggled the brick before removing it. He shifted

closer and peered into the hole. "There is a gap between here and the outer wall of the chimney. But there is not one behind the first brick we removed. That indicates to me that something has been bricked into the back of the fireplace and those new bricks packed in around it."

The anticipation was almost too much to bear. Jane nodded. "Let's keep going."

Ten minutes later, they had taken another half-dozen of the chocolate-colored bricks from the fireplace, leaving only one of them untouched. Tears threatened. If there had been a box of treasures, they should have found it by now.

George chipped around the edge of the last brick and yanked it free. It fell onto the floor and broke in two. "Oh," he murmured.

"Bricks don't normally do that do they?" she asked.

George picked up one half of the brick and examined it before handing it to Jane. "The middle is hollow, and there is something stuck in it. I think you should be the one to take it out."

She frowned as she caught a glimpse of a piece of folded yellowed paper. This was not a cache of jewels or gold.

Oh no.

With a sinking heart, Jane carefully withdrew the paper then unfolded it. There were a number of lines of writing at the top, all of which blurred with her tears.

"What does it say?" asked George, his voice still heavy with hope.

"It's another of King Charles's bloody letters offering to give Jane Whorwood a good, hard ride in bed." She slumped to the floor, screwing up the piece of paper in her hand. "Why the devil would she have gone to all that trouble just to hide a love letter? It makes no sense at all," she grumbled.

George picked up the other half of the brick, giving it a glance before tossing it aside. "Who knows? Perhaps she thought it could harm the royal cause if their affair ever came to light."

"Perhaps, but if that was the case, she could have simply burned it."

He offered her his hand, but Jane shook her head. She didn't want comfort. Even the thought of being held in George's arms couldn't stir her interest.

There was no room left for consolation in her heart. It was already full to the brim with the shards of broken disappointment.

Chapter Twenty-Six

George had dealt with many dangerous and awkward situations in his life, but a disillusioned Jane was beyond even his well-honed set of skills. She sat across from him at the table, staring at the piece of paper for the best part of twenty minutes, refusing to talk.

She had pinned her whole future on the possibility of finding the treasure. He couldn't imagine how she must be feeling right now.

"There are other places we haven't looked yet," he offered.

She lifted her head and gave him a weary look—one which said his efforts to placate her were in vain. They had both gotten their hopes up this afternoon. The moment the brick had fallen apart in his hands, George had sensed the familiar rush of adrenaline. He had welcomed the dry sensation in his mouth. The lure of hidden treasure had him firmly in its grip.

But you didn't spend all those long hours in the British museum searching for the letters, and you have never been alone like her.

Despite his best intentions, he too had placed all his hopes and dreams for a different life in that one piece of paper.

And then nothing.

All they had to show for their long hours of hard work was a note from a reckless king seeking to gain sexual favors from one of his female courtiers. That, and a ruin of a house.

The situation felt hopeless. He was falling for Jane just as her hopes for success were crumbling.

Jane is crushed by this, and there is nothing I can do to make it better.

He got to his feet. "I am going to go for a stroll and try to clear my head. I'll lock the door behind me."

Jane gave the merest of nods as he walked away.

George had never realized how hard it could be to reach another person—doubly so now that he was trying to build a bond with Jane. An unbreakable one that would see their lives permanently fused together.

But as he stepped into the busy and crowded Drury Lane, he found himself fresh out of ideas as to what he should do.

He had never encountered any problems when making friends with men. The strength of the ties which bound the rogues of the road together had been forged in the blistering heat of war and danger. Nothing could break them apart.

Jane, however, was an entirely different conundrum. An enigma he had no idea as to how he could unravel.

How many women would offer themselves up to a gentleman like him and not expect an offer of marriage? According to his way of thinking, she should have demanded one the second they had finished making love for the first time. But Jane hadn't. In fact, she had made her thoughts on the subject quite clear. She didn't see a future with him.

"Blast," he muttered.

What was she thinking saying that to him? A chap could take offense at being told not to bother proposing to a woman.

With hands stuffed into his coat pockets, he continued south, grumbling and whispering to himself. He really ought to go home and see his parents—let them know that he was at least alive.

But they will want to know how things are going with you and young Toby. Remember that lie?

That was not a good idea. He was tired of lying to people.

A body stepped into his path, and George went to move around it. The figure followed his steps and he glanced up. A word of reproach was ready at his lips.

"By Jove you look a misery," said Augustus Jones.

He managed a tight smile for his fellow RR Coaching Company director, then sighed. "When did you get back to town?"

"Stephen and I were only gone two nights. Down to Portsmouth and then home again. Once we had Lisandro and Maria onboard my yacht, we started on the return journey," said Gus.

A Spanish duke and a kidnapped noblewoman in England. Now there was a story George was keen to hear the sordid details of over a brandy or three.

"What are you doing in this part of town? I didn't think you ever frequented Drury Lane unless you were headed to the theatre in the evening," said George.

Gus pointed back in the direction from which George had just come. "I was on my way to see you. Harry was rather vague about what you and that lovely antiquities girl were doing with the house you bought, so I thought a visit was in order."

George didn't want to tell Gus that he and Jane were on a treasure hunt. The less people who knew the truth the better.

"Actually, that's a lie. I was coming to talk to you because I have a little job which I think would suit you perfectly," said Gus.

"I'm afraid I don't intend on doing any more, *little* jobs. I am going straight," replied George.

"Bah! Nonsense. You are a rogue thief at heart. I've seen the look on your face when smuggled cargo lands on the beach. You are like a child on Christmas Eve. Come on, grumpy guts. Show me your new house and then I can finally meet Jane Scott," he said, continuing on his way.

Your timing couldn't be any worse. I'm sure the last thing Jane wants is a visitor.

Gus was headed toward Coal Yard Lane, leaving George with no other option than to scamper after him.

Back at the house, they found Jane still seated at the table, staring at the love letter. When Gus walked into the kitchen, she startled and quickly rose from her chair, stuffing the paper into her skirts.

"Relax. This is Gus," said George.

Gus, being his usual self, bowed low. "Augustus Trajan Jones at your service, Miss Scott."

A clearly unimpressed Jane held out her hand. "There is no need for such formalities, Gus; George has explained about your professional occupation. Or, should I say, line of business? As for the grubby bits which your fellow, rogue of the road, accidently on purpose left out, Lady Alice was kind enough to impart them to me. I have no illusions."

Gus righted himself and gave a questioning sideways stare at George. "What exactly did you tell her? And what did Alice say?"

For the first time since they had found the letter, Jane managed a smile. George let out a small sigh of relief.

"George told me that you have a beautiful yacht called *the Nightwind*—a vessel which you use to smuggle goods into England. I am yet to meet any friends of George who are not up to their eyeballs in illegal activities," replied Jane.

Gus gave a dirty chuckle. "Ah, now I understand why Alice Steele thinks you are the best thing to ever happen to

George. You have this blackguard's measure. Promise me you will marry this rascal and make an honest man of him."

Jane slowly shook her head. "I'm afraid you all have it wrong. George and I are merely business partners. Once this private venture is over, I expect he will go back to his old life, and I shall move on with mine."

The spark of hope which had flared in George's heart at Gus's demand for Jane to marry him was instantly snuffed out. She had no intention of ever being his.

Chapter Twenty-Seven

"So much for you promising to change your ways and live the life of an honest man," said Jane.

She wasn't even going to pretend that she was happy about him disappearing with Gus to a mysterious locale somewhere along the Kentish coast. They were smuggling in contraband, and that was all she needed to know. It set her temper to boiling point.

I am not going to ask them anything else. I really don't want to know.

He sighed. "This was not of my choosing. Gus needs my help. Stephen is busy working a case for one of his clients. Monsale is still in the country, and there is no one else who can go."

"What about Harry or is he too good for that sort of work?" she replied.

The fifth member of the rogues of the road never seemed to get his hands dirty.

"Harry only deals with the legitimate side of the business these days. Alice had that condition included as part of the marriage contract. If he ever touches anything illegal, she can cut him off without a penny."

Clever girl. She is trying to protect her man.

From the time she had spent with Alice, Jane had learned enough of the woman to know she would make good on that threat if Lord Harry ever decided to be foolish.

"Gus will need to look for someone else going forward. That is if you are serious about changing your ways. Or perhaps you are not," she replied.

"I have made a commitment to Gus, and I am going to keep it. The only thing you need to concern yourself about is staying away from leery shopkeepers," he bit back.

She shot him an irritated scowl. This argument was giving her a headache. "I am perfectly safe here. And I will keep the loaded pistol with me at all times. I promise that if at any point during your absence I don't feel right in staying at the house, I shall decamp to Harry and Alice's home. Is that enough for you?" said Jane.

George cleared his throat. "I will be back in a week. In the meantime, just try and keep a low profile."

In the years since her family had died, Jane had learned to take care of herself. It was annoying to hear a man deliver such rigid instructions—especially when he had no legal standing over her.

As if you have any right to tell me what to do. I am the one who decides my life.

"Please," he added.

Her shoulders sagged as the last of the fight fled her. This was a pointless argument she was never going to win. "Alright. While I wait for you to return, I will keep searching through the house for any other clues. I don't believe that a simple love letter could have been enough to keep Jane Whorwood interested in this house. There has to be more to it than that," she replied.

God, please let there be more. I can't have wasted all that time over nothing.

George set his bag on the floor of the parlor and pulled

Jane into his embrace. She accepted the soft kiss he placed on her lips, then returned the favor when he gave her his puppy dog eyes. No woman could refuse a man when he wielded those sorts of weapons.

"You might think that I am being overbearing," he said.

"Which you are."

He growled. "But I care about you. And I don't just mean your health and well-being. Will you promise to do something for me while I am away?"

Demanding male. "What?"

"I need you to give serious consideration to what Gus said about our relationship, to what a life together could be like for the two of us. While I am as keen as you are to find hidden treasure, we have to consider what we will do if we discover that it was all just a myth." He took her hand in his and linked their fingers. "The lack of a king's fortune doesn't have to be the end of things between us, Jane. We could be married."

She wanted to argue the point about the existence of the jewel hoard, but as he was about to walk out the door and into lord knew what danger, now was not the right time. As to the rest of his request, she really wasn't sure what she thought.

Perhaps he is right and now is the time to ponder what future we might have, if any.

"I will think about us. But that does not mean I have agreed to anything. Just because we are lovers, doesn't mean you own me, George." She withdrew her hand from his grasp but remained in his embrace.

He leaned in and kissed her once more. "I would never seek to own you, Jane Scott. If you are by my side, it is because that is exactly where you want to be."

With George gone, Jane had expected the house to feel cold and soulless. Oddly, it didn't. Over the next day or so, she spent many hours moving from room to room, looking into nooks and crannies, while at the same time, she started cleaning.

By late afternoon on the second day of his absence, Jane had swept and mopped the floors, dusted windowsills, and was giving serious consideration as to what she should do with the calico drapes which hung in the bedrooms.

As she stood pondering the fate of the dusty curtains in the master bedroom, she was struck with a sudden realization. A hand went instinctively to her stomach.

"I am nesting," she whispered.

She and George had made love a number of times. Before and after each sexual encounter, she had been careful to make use of the acacia and honey cream she had purchased from an apothecary shop in nearby Eagle Street. She had utilized it as a form of contraception while in Malta, and it had worked, but even Jane knew such things were not completely infallible. She swallowed deeply in an effort to calm herself.

"Don't panic. It is just your heart wanting a home, nothing more."

And what if it's not? What if you are . . .

She couldn't even think the word, let alone say it. But her mind quickly moved to the image of Lady Alice Steele, of how she glowed with happiness every time Lord Harry touched her heavily pregnant belly.

If she and George did make a future together, this place could be their family home. It wasn't in the best part of London, but it would do for a start. Without the treasure, it would be more than she could ever hope to have, then again, it could be everything.

"Damn."

Jane wiped away a tear. Just the notion of being a part of a family once more was almost too much for her emotions to bear.

But you would finally have to acknowledge your feelings for him. And willingly place your trust in the hands of a man who has lived a life of secrets, lies, and thievery. A man who has sworn to change, but who is most likely engaged in an operation to smuggle illegal imports into England right this very minute.

"No. I will not think about that today. I have other things to occupy my mind."

She turned and headed downstairs, but with every step she took, Jane could not ignore the whispers of her heart.

This could be your home, and George your future.

Chapter Twenty-Eight

"I like Jane Scott," said Gus. George frowned at him from the other side of the carriage.

Where did that sudden thought come from? Or was it sudden? The fact that Gus was even thinking about Jane set George's temper on edge.

I knew I shouldn't have introduced the two of them.

"I also happen to like Jane, so stay the hell away from her," snapped George.

Gus clapped his hands together with great glee. "Ah, my friend. Cupid has stuck a sharp arrow in your arse. If you had bothered to check yourself in a mirror when I came to your home, you would know the look which sat on your face when I met sweet Jane."

"And what look is that exactly?" replied George, knowing full well he didn't need to study his own reflection.

"The same mawkish expression that Harry has on his stupid visage every time he sneaks a glance in the direction of his wife. Even our Spanish friend Lisandro wore it when he looked at Maria. All this love. It is such a sweet thing to observe," said Gus.

George silently wished he had some witty retort which he

could aim in the direction of his friend, but he had none. Gus had spoken the truth.

He was in love with Jane. Irrefutably, irrevocably, and to the deepest depths of his soul. The only problem being that he wasn't entirely sure about her feelings toward him. If she didn't reciprocate his affections, then unrequited love was going to be a beast he had to constantly battle.

Jane was a woman who not only enjoyed sex but who also didn't appear to place an emotional attachment to it. And while this had been all well and good with the other women whose beds George had shared, it certainly wasn't the same case with her. Why? Because he was in love.

Bloody hell, I want her to love me back. And I need her to trust me.

George rubbed his hands over his tired face. They had many hours of work still ahead of them before *the Nightwind* arrived on the late tide and anchored in the remote Kentish cove. For the first time in the many years since he had worked with his friend's smuggling operations, he found himself struggling to summon any real interest in whatever valuables were onboard the yacht.

And that was a dangerous state of mind for any criminal to find himself in.

"This is my last job. Please don't ask me to do this again, because the answer will be no. Harry managed to walk away from a life of crime, and I am determined to do the same."

Gus shifted and came to sit beside him. "Alright. How about you take the rifle and keep guard at the top of the road leading down to the cove? That should be an easy enough task. And after tonight, I will consider you officially retired from the smuggling business."

George gave a resigned nod. There was a job to do, a commitment to see Gus's cargo ashore. Handling a rifle was about the limit of his attention span at the moment. His mind was mostly concerned with Jane and his regret over having left her.

I won't ever do that again.

"Alright. Let's get this piece of mischief managed and then I will officially call it a day on my wicked ways." George reached for the rifle, which he had stowed under the seat. One more night of handling contraband and he was done.

Now he just had to make it safely back to London and get Jane to willingly accept that he was the man for her.

Chapter Twenty-Nine

❦

Jane finished the last of her fish breakfast from the seafood monger in Covent Garden. They unfortunately didn't sell whitebait, but the piece of fried cod she got was particularly delicious and that countered any real sense of disappointment she might have felt. With a full stomach, she rested at the kitchen table, unwilling to move.

Eventually, she would have to get up and continue her search of the house, but for the moment she was content to sit and daydream.

Her gaze drifted to the note King Charles had written to Jane Whorwood. The old, yellowed paper had sat on the table for the past few days. She picked it up and read it yet again.

"Why would she hide this? People must have known that they were lovers. And he was already being held a prisoner at Carisbrooke Castle when she hid this letter. There was no way he was going to be released."

The note itself was very short, leaving much of the paper on which it had been written blank.

She stared at it for a time. Her eyes focused on the large, unused section. Jane Whorwood had acted as King Charles's secret agent. A spy for the crown.

What if there is something else on the page? Something the naked eye can't see.

If there were secrets hidden within the paper, how was she to unlock them?

"Invisible ink. Could that be it?"

The Persians and Ottomans alike had used various chemicals to hide messages in fabric. It was nothing new. A reagent of some sort was always required to reveal the hidden writing. Where in London would she find such a thing?

It was a stab in the dark. Probably yet another dead end in a long series of them, but she had to try.

Half an hour later, with her hair brushed and wearing her best coat, Jane walked as casually as her thumping heart would allow into the famous Ackermann's Repository of Arts at 101 the Strand. She had heard of the legendary shop which sold prints, books, and art materials, but had never before ventured through its front door.

She was still rehearsing what she should say when a well-dressed middle-aged man approached. He bowed. "Good morning. Welcome to Ackermann's. How may I assist you?"

She bit back a grin. The formal way that the people who worked in London shops addressed her had always struck Jane as amusing.

In Byblos they would have spat on the ground and then shoved a goat at you, demanding that you haggle for it.

"I am not sure how to explain this—I wish to play a game with a friend. He wants to be able to send me a note, but it has to be in secret. There is nothing untoward about any of what we are doing; it's just for a spot of amusement," she explained.

A sparkle glinted in the man's eye. "And, of course, you would want to be able to read what your gentleman friend has written?"

When Jane nodded, he gestured for her to follow him.

This looks promising.

At a large wooden counter, the shop assistant produced two glass jars. One contained a pale brown liquid, which looked like a cup of weak tea. The other jar contained a yellowish liquid.

Is that urine?

"Now, these are the two main components you need for sending secret letters," he explained.

He pointed at the brown jar. "That is oak gall, made by soaking gall nuts for four days. Your friend writes his note using it. Then he waits for the paper or fabric to dry. It writes invisibly. Then, he sends it to you."

"And how do I retrieve the note?" she asked, fascinated.

He pointed at the second jar and smiled. "You dip a brush in that liquid, which is iron sulfate, then carefully wipe it over the paper. His words will magically appear."

Could it be that simple? Please Lord, let it be.

"And this is something that people have always used?" she enquired.

"Well, yes, because it is how most ink is made. All you are doing is separating the two compounds at the beginning. This method of sending secret messages was used extensively during the English Civil War. It was how Charles the First's supporters used to write letters and evade Cromwell's men. Quite ingenious, don't you think?"

"Why, yes, it is. Could you perhaps sell me a jar of each please?" she replied.

He smiled knowingly at her. "Certainly. One must aid communications between friends as best as one can."

Jane left the shop a short time later with two well-sealed jars and a small paint brush in her possession. The fond farewell she received from the shop assistant warmed her heart. It was lovely to meet someone who no doubt thought he might be playing a small but vital role in helping the way of young love.

Back at Coal Yard Lane, she closed the front door and locked it. She took two steps toward the kitchen, then went back to make certain the door was closed fast. If she was about to unveil the secrets of the treasure, the last thing she needed was to have unexpected and unwelcome visitors.

George would kill me.

Her hands were trembling as she placed the jars onto the table and reached into her pocket for the note. She set the tea-colored oak gall ink to one side before unscrewing the lid of the jar containing the yellow iron sulfate.

And then she paused for a moment—first to send a prayer to her father in heaven, then to hold a special thought for George.

"I wish you were both here," she whispered.

She swallowed a lump of tension then, after picking up the brush, she dipped it into the liquid. The first stroke across the paper had her gasping. Two words magically appeared.

My love.

A single tear snaked down her cheek as she went back to the jar and soaked up more of the reagent.

Five minutes later, Jane sat staring at the words which had been hidden for over one hundred and sixty years.

> **My love's greatest treasure be**
> **Not under stars or moon**
> **The one true heir did tarry here**
> **As does this royal boon.**

She slumped in the chair. "It's a bloody cypher. Oh, Jane, why couldn't you just have said 'X' marks the spot? It would make my life so much easier."

Knowing that the treasure was real meant she could somewhat forgive her namesake. The task which lay ahead of her was to decode the message.

Simple enough. Or not.

She read the rhyme a second time.

"Who the devil was the one true heir?"

Her fingers drummed on the table while she wracked her brains. *Thrump. Thrump.*

"It's obvious we are talking about the British throne, which means . . . oh!"

If the note had been written by Jane Whorwood after Charles the First had been removed from the throne, then the true heir should have been his son. Parliament had proclaimed Charles the Second King of England some eleven years after his father's execution.

She got to her feet and excitedly waved the paper about. This moment called for a little jig on the spot. The first part of the riddle had been solved.

After placing the drying note back on the table, Jane focused her attention on what she knew of Charles the Second.

Scoundrel and unashamed adulterer. Fathered at least a dozen illegitimate children. Loved a good party. Popular king. Known as the Merry Monarch.

"No. That would have come later. What else? Think, Jane."

Yet again, her attention returned to the note. "So, Charles the Second must have stayed at a particular place and that is where the treasure is buried?"

Her hopes dimmed.

After his father's arrest, the younger Charles and the rest of the royal family had left England for the safety of the continent. The future king had returned later and tried to claim the throne but had been defeated at the Battle of Worcester, after which he had fled the country once more.

"And after Worcester, he was on the run, during which time he famously had to hide up a tree at Boscobel House in Shropshire," she muttered.

If the boon had indeed been buried, then it wouldn't be under stars or moon. What if Jane Whorwood had buried the treasure where the future king had taken refuge before his flight from England?

The pieces of the puzzle were beginning to fall into place.

But why Jane Whorwood would have chosen Boscobel House as the place to bury the treasure wasn't so clear. Shropshire was a long way from London, and it would necessitate a special trip for anyone who sought to retrieve the treasure.

Which makes even more sense now that I think about it. By hiding it far away, no one would accidently stumble upon it.

The Royal Oak Tree at Boscobel House may well have held the secret of the royal treasure for many years; now it might also hold Jane's fate in its leafy green hands.

"I have to go to Shropshire."

If she took the fast mail coach headed to Holyhead via Birmingham, and then alighted at Shrewsbury, she could possibly make it to Boscobel House in a day or two. Allowing for time to dig around the tree, hopefully locating the treasure and making good on the return journey, she could be back in London in under a week.

What about George?

She should really wait for his return. He would expect it.

"Yes, well he didn't hesitate to disappear off to Kent. There was no consideration as to what I thought of him helping Gus handle smuggled goods, was there?" she muttered.

George had spoken of giving up his criminal ways, but it would appear that old habits die hard.

After retrieving the note, Jane folded it in two. Her mind was made up.

At first light she fully intended to be on the doorstep of the *Swan with Two Necks* in Lad Lane, and once inside, she would purchase herself a return ticket to Shrewsbury. If

George Hawkins had any problem with her plans, he could take it up with her once she got back.

I've made no promises to him. He hasn't any right to be angry with me.

And if she did return to London with a king's secret treasure in her possession, she was certain all would be forgiven.

Chapter Thirty

❧

Three days later

George wasn't angry—he was livid.

"Bloody hell, where are you?" he grumbled.

The scant note Jane had left crumpled in his fist.

Following a clue. All may not be lost. J.S.

He would give a gold coin right now for a blazing fire into which he could throw Jane's piece of nonsense and stand back to watch while it burned. His instructions had been clear; she was to remain at the house and await his return.

Instead, she had gone *lord knew where* in search of the treasure—a fanciful bounty that George had finally accepted likely didn't exist.

"Pig-headed, intractable, stubborn . . . *woman*."

The moment Jane returned; George was going to have firm words with her. He would take her in hand and show her just who was in charge.

"And then you will start doing what you are told," he huffed.

Or at least I hope so.

⁂

Several days later, George was seated at the table, still steaming over Jane's sudden disappearance, when the front door clicked shut and a moment later, she walked into the kitchen. One look at her crestfallen face had him biting back the words of rebuke which had sat bitterly on his tongue since his return home. "Jane?"

She shook her head and promptly burst into tears.

All thoughts of giving her a stern lecture were cast aside as George took Jane into his arms and wrapped her up in his embrace. He would have it out with her later. All that was important was that she was home, and she was safe.

Thank God.

He placed gentle kisses on the top of Jane's light brown hair. This was what really mattered—holding the woman he loved in his arms while she cried all over him.

⁂

"One hundred and thirty odd miles there, and the same all the way back, with yet again nothing to show for my efforts," lamented Jane.

Her shoulders and hips ached from long hours tightly crammed in with the other passengers in the mail coach. She hadn't slept a wink on the return journey. The gentleman seated next to her had liked to spread his elbows and knees, leaving her little room to move.

"Yes, but you discovered the secret of the note, which is quite a feat in itself." George was seated next to her on the mattress in the parlor, a blanket thrown over their legs for warmth. He held the cryptic letter in his hand.

She could sense he was aching to give her a right bollocking over her having disappeared and gone all the way to the Welsh border on her own, but he was holding his temper. Her tears had done much to calm her emotions, but disappointment had left a nasty taste in her mouth.

"So, tell me what happened when you arrived at Boscobel House," he said.

Jane lay her head against the parlor wall and closed her eyes. Apart from the drudgery of a protracted coach journey, there wasn't much to report. "I got all the way to Boscobel House and found that the tree was gone. Apparently, Charles the Second's exploits of hiding in the oak tree were more famous than I had realized. In the years after it happened, hundreds of people came and took souvenirs of the original tree. And, of course, it eventually died. They dug it up, thus disproving my theory of Jane Whorwood having buried the treasure around the base."

Using an acorn from the original, another royal oak tree had been grown nearby. It too garnered a solid number of daily visitors all milling around its base. Even if she had wanted to dig, Jane would never have been able to manage a time when she was alone.

"And that's when I realized I had gone off in search of something that doesn't exist. If the treasure had been buried at that spot, I expect someone would have found it long ago and kept it a secret."

A warm hand took hold of one of hers, and she opened her eyes. When she chanced a look in George's direction, her heart did a little flip. He was softly smiling at her. "You did what you could. Jane, I am sorry you didn't find the treasure. After all you have been though, if anyone deserves to have found the boon, it is you."

Jane shifted and rose up on her knees. George placed his hands on either side of her hips as she straddled him. "I don't want to talk about it anymore tonight. I just want you," she whispered.

A gentle hand was placed at the back of her head and he drew her to him. The heady sensation of his lips and mouth on hers soon had Jane thinking of nothing else but giving herself to this man. Their tongues settled to tease and play in a familiar, welcome dance.

It had only been a matter of days since they had last been together, but she ached with need for his touch.

"Will you let me make love to you?" he asked.

Stubborn and tenacious he might be, but George had never once taken without first asking her permission. He cared about her—showed it in all manner of ways that truly mattered.

Tears pricked at her eyes, but this time they were ones born of joy.

"I've missed you," she said. She received a long, loving kiss as a reward.

"So, have I. I've missed holding you, loving you. This bed has been so bloody empty over the past few nights. Promise you won't ever disappear on me like that again. I couldn't stand it," he said.

Her fingers reached between them, and she flicked open the top button on the placket of his trousers. A simple *yes* wouldn't suffice. Tonight, she wanted to show George that he wasn't the only one invested in this relationship.

Taking his hard cock in hand, she began to stroke the long length. On a needful groan, George closed his eyes.

"I promise you won't ever have to sleep here alone again." She shimmied down the bed, coming to a halt when she reached the point where she was facing his erect manhood. George speared his fingers into Jane's hair as she took him into her mouth and began to suck. The soft echoes of his groans were soon the only sounds in the room.

The missing treasure of a long-dead king might have eluded her, but Jane Scott was finally determined that this magnificent prize would be hers.

Chapter Thirty-One

The one true heir did tarry here.

Jane lay on her back staring up at the dark ceiling, the words of the short rhyme rolling continually around in her head. The letter had to mean something. No one in their right mind would have bothered to write a note, then seal it up behind the bricks of the fireplace unless they'd intended for it to serve some purpose.

Disappointment over the journey to Boscobel House sat heavy in her heart. She had set out from London with such great hope, only to see it all come to naught.

Her other reason for being awake at such an ungodly hour was sound asleep beside her on the mattress, snoring gently.

At least one of us is getting some rest.

Their lovemaking earlier had been all that she craved. George hadn't let her bring him to completion with her mouth. Instead, he had rolled Jane onto her back and thrust deep into her heated core. He had ridden her to an earth-shattering climax.

Absolute bliss.

If he had any idea as to how masterful he was in giving sexual pleasure to a woman, George hid it well. He was a generous lover, always taking his cue from her sobs and groans. When she'd clutched at his hips, desperate for release, he'd shifted position and ground against her clit. Her world had been filled with shooting stars as it exploded.

Now, lying next to him in the dark, she let her mind consider the question of what lay ahead for the two of them.

What was she to do about George? He had hinted at marriage more than once.

But what would a marriage between us look like?

She had trusted one man with her future and been betrayed, and despite what her heart was pleading for her to do, she wasn't going to rush into making that mistake a second time. There were long conversations to be had before any final decision was made.

Doing her best not to disturb George and his restful slumber, Jane rose from the mattress and headed through the kitchen and out to the rear garden. There was a full moon tonight, and it bathed the world in an eerie, silver light.

After using the privy, she wandered back toward the house, stopping for a moment while she further pondered her options.

What if I don't stay with him? What if George is not willing to give up his life of crime? If that's the case, then I cannot see us having a future. I will not bind myself to a man who may end his days at the end of a hangman's noose.

There were other avenues she could pursue. She could, of course, seek a new role as a governess or perhaps a lady's companion. Neither option appealed but being alone would mean she had to make her own way in the world. She'd need money and a place to live.

When it came to George, there was still the issue of trust. Once bit, twice shy. It sounded like a well-worn cliché, but it held a world of truth.

"If I could just get some sleep, I might be able to make better sense of all this," she muttered.

She reached out and placed her hand on the gnarled old oak tree that grew in the rear garden, patting it while she pondered her life's predicament. Tearing a leaf from one of the lower hanging branches, Jane flattened it out in the palm of her hand. She sighed as she traced her fingertip along the center midrib of the leaf before screwing it up and tossing it onto the ground.

One.

Two.

She was three steps closer to the door when she suddenly stopped, whirled around, and stared up at the oak tree.

The oak tree.

She dashed inside and into the parlor. She dropped onto the mattress and shook George roughly by the shoulder. "George! Wake up!"

He rolled over and cracked open an eyelid. "What? I was having a wonderful dream about baked salmon and roast potatoes. Why would you wake me?"

She shook him again, not convinced that he was yet fully awake enough to register her words. "Quick. Get dressed," she ordered.

Jane didn't know whether to laugh or cry.

He batted her hand away and sat up, blinking into the semi-darkness. The blanket fell as he rummaged around on the mattress, finally picking up his shirt. "This had better be good," he grumbled, slipping it over his head.

"An oak tree. The heir tarried in an oak tree. That's where the treasure is," she babbled.

The scowl on George's face was evident even in the poor light. Placing his hands either side of her face, he looked into her eyes. "Jane, are you sleepwalking? Is it you who needs to be woken?"

She pulled back, flapping her arms about excitedly. "I couldn't be more awake if I tried. I assumed the oak tree was *the* tree at Boscobel House, the one in which Charles the Second hid from the parliamentarian forces."

He sighed. "But you went to Shropshire. The treasure wasn't there!"

She leaned in close, so that their faces were a mere inch apart, and grinned at him. "George, there is an oak tree in the garden of *this* house."

He seized Jane's arm. "Get dressed. Get the lantern. I'll find the pickaxe. Jane, we need to dig around the base of the tree!"

She leaned in and kissed him sweetly on the lips. "Indeed, we do, my love."

George clambered to his feet. He put on his trousers and picked up his boots. At the same time, Jane hurriedly dressed.

As she stepped past him, headed for the door, George took Jane by the hand and pulled her back. She spun into his embrace. "Oh, what?"

"You just called me my love," he said.

"Did I?"

He bent his head and kissed her long and deeply. They really should have been out in the dark digging for the treasure, but Jane couldn't muster the will to protest. She pressed herself flush against his hard, manly body.

When George finally released her, they were both panting heavily. "You know you did, which leaves only one question. And that's when are you going to say it again?"

Jane was relieved that in the dim light George couldn't see the heat that burned her cheeks.

He kissed her one last time before leading her toward the door.

I will say it when you do.

Chapter Thirty-Two

The soil at the base of the oak tree was harder than George had anticipated. The second the pickaxe struck the ground it made a loud *whomp* noise. In the still night air, the sound created a loud and worrying echo. Anyone who was awake in the dozen or so closely clustered houses of Coal Yard Lane would surely have heard it.

"Bloody hell. We will have half the neighborhood knocking on our door if we try and dig," Jane muttered.

George nodded. "You had better kill that light just to be safe. The last thing we need is prying eyes."

Jane lifted the glass of the lamp she was holding and immediately blew out the candle. "Come back inside, and let's decide on what's to be done," she whispered.

He had undertaken enough dirty jobs in the dark to know that one didn't risk waking the local inhabitants. People who'd been stirred from sleep tended to be both grumpy and nosey.

Back in the kitchen, while Jane sat at the table and relit the lamp, George paced the floor. No one suggested that they go back to bed; there was not a chance that either of them would get any sleep.

He forced himself to focus on the job at hand, not Jane's earlier revelation. Her declaration of love, if it could be called one, had moved him more deeply than he could ever have imagined it would. A woman coming into his life and shaking up his whole world was something George Hawkins hadn't thought possible.

And yet Jane Scott had done exactly that.

Think! Concern your thoughts with dealing with the dirt around the tree—then you can take the time to deal with Jane's affections.

"We are never going to be able to keep our efforts to dig in the garden a secret, especially if we attempt them at night," she said.

"Excavating during the day will also be problematic, but it might be easier. We just need a plausible reason to be messing about in the rear yard," he replied.

"Plenty of people around here have plots of land with home gardens. If anyone comes to the house, we could tell them we are going to reestablish the garden along with the herb and vegetable beds," replied Jane.

George nodded his agreement. "Good idea."

The story Jane proposed was a clever one. George had lived a long enough life of subterfuge and falsehoods to know that simple lies were usually the best.

"But we need to do something about the side fence. There are holes aplenty in it. Anyone could easily put their face up to one of the gaps and see that we were digging around the base of the tree," she said.

George stopped his incessant walking and dropped into the chair across the table from her. He raked his fingers through his tussled hair. The fence was a real problem. During the day there were plenty of people passing through the laneway which ran alongside the house. They didn't need an audience.

He leaned against the back of the chair and met Jane's

gaze. While her face was full of concern, there was also a spark of excitement gleaming in her eyes. There were obstacles for them to overcome, but if they could succeed in finding the treasure, it would be all worthwhile.

What if we did go ahead with the charade of planting a garden?

"Jane, I like your lie; it suits our purposes perfectly. We should do everything we can to make it look real. That way, if anyone does poke their head through the fence, all they are going to see is a young couple working to establish a garden. I can bring some horse manure over from the RR Coaching Company stables. As I dig up the dirt, you can work the fresh droppings through it. That way people will think you are making compost."

She nodded. "Could you also get some straw? I was thinking I could pull down the rotten calico curtains from upstairs and lay them over where we have been working at the end of each day, then toss the dry material on top so as to disguise any holes."

He smiled at her. Trust Jane to be thinking one step ahead of their problems. She was finding ways to address issues before they even arose. "Wisely and slow. They stumble that run fast," he replied.

"I am pleased to see that your education was not entirely wasted, George Hawkins. I like a man who can quote Shakespeare."

When this is all over, I am not letting you go.

"And you are a very clever young woman, Jane Scott. Have I told you that?"

"No. But thank you. While I do happen to have some belief in myself, it is still nice to hear it from another person," she replied.

If she gave him a chance, George would happily spend the rest of his life offering her up such tender and real compliments.

Restless and in need of distraction, he held out his hand to her. "I don't think either of us is getting any more sleep tonight. How about we go down to the River Thames and watch the sun rise? If you are a good girl, I will buy you some freshly baked rolls and a mug of hot chocolate."

Jane grinned at him. "That sounds wonderful. You, the dawn, and hot chocolate." Jane took his hand, and George was pleased when she eagerly accepted his kiss. When she finally drew back from his lips, their gazes met. A glint of mischief shone in her eyes. "I will have you know, George Hawkins, I am always a good girl, until I am not."

His manhood twitched at her suggestive tone and his appetite moved to a different sort of hunger. He ached with the need to have Jane naked and beneath him, writhing with pleasure. "Change of plans. Forget about the dawn—it will be there tomorrow. You and I are going to back to bed. We can worry about food later."

Her hand settled on his burgeoning erection, and all discussion was quickly at an end.

Chapter Thirty-Three

It didn't take long for the neighbors to find the goings on in the backyard of number eleven Coal Yard Lane to be of great interest. But to the collected disappointment of many, there had not been a mysterious body secretly buried during the night, nor even a new chicken hutch built. Words of frustration were muttered by several local residents at hearing the news that it was all simply in aid of a vegetable patch.

George was nothing if not the master of a well-practiced sleight of hand. Dull and boring were his weapons of choice when it came to unwelcome attention.

As soon as he and Jane were done with breakfast, George had ventured over to the RR Coaching Company offices with the intention of not only getting some manure and straw, but to offer up his apologies for his extended absence.

But when he got there, only Bob, the lone stable hand, and an odd-looking three-legged dog were about the place. All the other members of the company were missing.

The dog ambled over, and George bent and gave him a friendly pat. There were old, healed bite wounds on the animal's face.

You've had a hard life, my boy.

"And who is this?" he asked.

"That is Snick. He's Toby's dog. They rescued him during a recent piece of work. Apparently, his former owner had a run in with a bullet and a Spanish duke," replied Bob.

George didn't respond to the remark. It was RR Coaching Company policy not to discuss projects once they were completed. From the contented way the dog roamed the yard, it was obvious the unfortunate Snick had finally had a piece of luck in becoming the mascot for the rogues of the road. "Do you know where everyone has gone?" enquired George.

Bob shrugged. "Lord Harry took young Toby home with him this morning. Sir Stephen and Mister Augustus Jones hitched the horses to the small travel coach and went off on another job. I am not sure when they will be back."

George paused for a long second, adopting an air of indifference. It was time to remind Bob of the rules. "What else?"

The stable hand mimicked his expression. "Where they were going and what they were doing is, of course, none of my business. I am only a laborer, here to muck out the stables."

George nodded his approval at the well-rehearsed line. If anyone ever came to the coaching yard asking questions, that was all they were ever going to get.

He righted himself and gave Bob a pat on the back. "Good man. Now give me a hand with the manure, and I will get out of your way."

§

Taking the curtains down from the windows left Jane covered in filth, dust, and an eon's worth of cobwebs. She was still checking for spiders as she carried them out of the house and into the garden. It felt as if a hundred of the little black creatures were crawling all over her skin.

After dumping the pile of drapes on the ground, she

hurried over to where George was still unloading the cart full of straw and manure.

"Could you please have a look at the back of my gown and hair and make sure there are no spiders? You wouldn't believe how disgusting it was in those rooms, especially behind the curtains," she said.

He lay the shovel against the cart and sauntered over to her. "I thought you were tougher than that. Fancy letting a couple of spiders get you in a pickle."

Jane whirled round. "There are spiders? Get them off me!"

"Calm down. There aren't any on you." George brushed his hand over the top of her head. Jane squealed once more. The evil chuckle which he gave her earned him a hard punch on the arm.

"Beast," she said.

He leaned and kissed her on the forehead. "It is far too easy to get you all riled up. I thought I was hot tempered, but you, sweetheart, are always on the simmer."

She offered him her mouth, and he captured her lips in a long, lingering kiss. They might have a long afternoon of work ahead of them, but that didn't mean they couldn't tease and jest with one another.

"As I recall, last night you were the one who said he liked me being all ablaze. Or is that only when I am naked and riding your cock," she purred.

George groaned. "Don't talk like that. Not unless you want me to throw you over my shoulder, march back into the house, and take you to bed right this very minute."

She kissed him one last time before pulling away. "We have work to do. And besides, you don't deserve any sexual favors after that little jest about spiders." Jane laughed. She had never seen a man pout before.

He nibbled on her ear, then whispered, "How about I strip you naked later and use my lips and tongue to check in all your nooks and crannies—just to be sure that you are completely insect free?"

"That sounds delightful. But just for your edification, I will have you know that spiders are not insects."

He harrumphed, clearly not the least bit interested in the subject of entomology. "Bugs and all manner of crawling things are much the same to me, eight-legged or not. But you — well you, I find to be a source of endless fascination."

🙰

With a good area of the garden soil now disturbed, the pretense of planting new crops had been well established. Anyone who did happen to pass by in the lane would only see a man and woman preparing the ground for seedlings.

It was close to dusk when George headed over to the tree. With pickaxe in hand, he knelt and began to dig.

From her vantage point near the door, Jane kept an eye out for any passing busybodies, ready to engage them in idle conversation if needed.

A while later she came and stood closer to him.

"Anything?" she asked.

"No, the surface seems pretty even all round. But if something was actually buried here it might take time to unearth it. You have to remember there has been over one hundred odd years of weeds and ground movement in that time."

When she didn't reply, he glanced up at her. The expression of worry and impatience which showed on Jane's face took him by surprise.

He had foolishly assumed he was the one with his heart and soul on the line; her look was a sharp reminder that Jane was just as much, if not more, invested in the outcome of their search as him.

Of course, she is. This was her quest long before you came along. And before that it was a fanciful idea in her father's mind.

"Come here," he said.

She knelt beside him, and George put an arm around her. "I know this means a lot to you, but I want you to remember that it doesn't have to be everything. If we find the treasure, we do. If we don't, we will be disappointed, but we shall survive. And when I say we, I mean you and me."

You are worth more to me than all the treasures of the sultans and kings.

Jane let out a tired sigh, which stabbed like a sharp dagger straight to George's heart.

"I can't be with you, George, if that means living a life with a man who is a thief. I love you, but please don't ask that of me," she replied.

A tide of emotion so strong and resolute that only weeks ago George would have thought it impossible to experience welled up within him. Now he gladly accepted it. He had Jane's love, and that was his everything. This woman held the key to his heart, to his future.

He shifted and turned to face her. "I love you too. And I swear that I am going to walk away from my past. I told Gus when we were on the road to Kent that it was my last job for him, and I meant it."

If Harry could distance himself from that life, so could he. The tears that glistened in Jane's eyes gave him hope, but he needed more.

"Tell me you believe me. And if you don't, then what do I need to do to convince you?" he said.

She reached out and took hold of his hand. Seeming to pay no heed to its dirty and dusty state, Jane raised it to her lips. A tender kiss was placed on the cracked middle knuckle. "I do believe you want to change. But where I grew up, a man is judged by his actions, not his words. It is only through them that your truth can be fully known. Don't offer me promises, George. Instead, show me the sort of man you want to become."

She was going to hold him to his vow. A vow George Hawkins was determined he would keep.

Chapter Thirty-Four

The light was fading when Jane headed back into the house and washed up an hour later. While she went to a nearby shop and purchased two hot beef pies for their supper, George remained behind, tidying things up.

She ached all over. Muscles which had not seen much use since the days when she worked alongside her father at the archeological dig at Byblos Castle now painfully reminded Jane that she had lived a more sedentary life over the past few years.

If we do make a go of things and stay at this house, I will have to learn to work the garden properly.

George was tossing the last of the straw on top of the calico ground covers when she wandered back into the garden. "Did you want to wash your hands and come and eat while the pies are still hot?" Jane chuckled at her own words. *I sound like a housewife calling my husband in for his evening meal.*

George gave his clothes a quick dusting down then headed over. He leaned in and gifted Jane a tender kiss.

She went to step back, thinking he would follow her into the house, but he took a firm hold of her arm. "I didn't want to finish things up, but one of the neighbors has been watching through the fence. If it looks like we are done for the day, hopefully she will get bored and go home."

"But there is nothing to see, is there? So why are you worried? she replied.

He drew her into his arms and kissed her once more. When the kiss ended, George didn't release Jane from his embrace. Rather, he blazed a trail of hot kisses up the side of her neck, then nibbled sweetly on her earlobe.

She shivered at the memory of his touch earlier that morning. Of his lips sucking hard on her nipple as he thrust into her one last time and came. "If you keep that up, the pies will go cold."

He snorted. "I don't give a damn about the pies. And I want that woman to bugger off because there *is* something to see." His grip on her tightened. "Stay in my arms, Jane. I might be giving up the criminal life, but that doesn't mean I can't put my career skills to good use. The trick with deception is to be boring and predictable. We are acting the same as any young married couple. Let's go into the house and we can watch from the window until she leaves."

Jane's mind was filled with a hundred questions, but she did as George asked and let him lead her back inside. They closed the door behind them.

"What is it?" she asked.

"Shh," he replied.

For the next five minutes, he stared out the kitchen window, his attention fixed firmly on the woman lurking outside in the laneway. When the woman finally moved away, Jane touched a hand to his arm.

George flinched and let out a soft startled gasp.

"Sorry," she said.

He shook his head. "It's alright. I was just making certain she was gone. Some people like nothing better than to have a good idle gawk, but unfortunately, they are also the ones you have to watch out for. They have a horrible tendency to remember crucial details when the authorities are sniffing around for evidence of a crime. I'd have money on that woman being willing to sell out her grandmother if there was a coin in it for her."

But whatever interest Jane might have had in their unwelcome guest, it was now gone. "What is the something you found?"

He stirred and turned from the window. The edge of a grin sat on George's lips.

"I was moving some of the soil over to smooth it down when my pickaxe struck something hard. I toed at it with my boot, and from where I stood, I could tell it wasn't a rock. I caught a glimpse of something grey. That was when I realized I had an audience."

She put a hand to her mouth. Could they have truly found the long-lost treasure? Tears pricked at her eyes.

Oh, Papa, I wish you were here.

"I know you are eager to go and dig up whatever it is but trust me. This is the exact moment when all those who practice the art of the crook take a deep breath and . . . wait," he said.

She scowled at him. How could he possibly be offering up words of caution when a king's treasure might only be the turning of a sod away? "Are you in jest?" she replied.

George's expression, however, remained impassive, and she caught a glimpse of the master thief in action. "No, I have never seen the humor in this line of work. If we go racing out there all in a fluster, it will attract attention."

"What are we going to do?"

George reached for one of the pies. "We wait for the last gasp of light, then we dig." He took a large bite out of his beef supper before gesturing for Jane to do the same.

With a sigh, she picked up her pie, but while George made short work of his, Jane merely nibbled on the edge of the crust.

Chapter Thirty-Five

It was a long, testing half-hour before the sun finally dipped below the horizon, and George and Jane made their way back out of the house and over to the oak tree. She was nervous, her mouth dry. When she instinctively reached for her ring once more, about to twist it round and round her finger, George laid his hand over hers and all movement came to a halt.

"Stop it. I know you are anxious, but I can't think if you are fidgeting like that," he said.

She drew in a deep breath. "Is this what it is like when you are about to do a job? I mean, when you came to the embassy that night, were you this on edge?"

"Yes, always. If your pulse is not racing and your senses not on high alert, that's when you make mistakes. I've never told you this, but just before I met you, I tried to rob an art gallery. I was so enamored with the painting I was attempting to steal that I almost managed to get myself shot," he replied.

"That must have been a magnificent painting," she replied.

He nodded. "A Titian. Need I say more?"

"Trust you to want to nab a Renaissance masterpiece.

Couldn't you have gone for something more sedate like a nice landscape?" she replied.

He scowled at her remark, then headed over to where he had been working.

With Jane keeping watch, he cleared a small patch of the straw and calico covering away from the base of the oak tree. Every so often she glanced back over her shoulder at him, silently hoping that any moment now he would lift up a large chest and out of it would tumble priceless jewels.

"Damn," he muttered.

"What?" she whispered.

"We need a light. I can't find where I saw that piece of grey earlier."

There was the temptation to suggest that they wait until morning, but Jane knew neither of them had that much patience left in reserve. They would risk a light.

She hurried back into the house, returning a short time later with the lamp. While Jane held up a section of the calico curtain, effectively blocking George from the view of anyone who happened to be in the lane, he lit the flame of the lantern.

While George dug, Jane watched the laneway.

A rustle at the fence-line had her peering feverishly into the dark. "Go away, puss," she hissed.

George stopped and glanced up at her.

"It's just one of the local stray cats," she said from over her shoulder.

He went back to digging. "There," he whispered.

George set the lamp on the ground, then blew out the light. Jane blinked for a moment, impatient for her eyes to become accustomed to the sudden darkness. All the while, she listened as George, unable to make use of the pickaxe, dug around in the dirt with his bare hands.

"It's the top of something. It feels like a metal box," he whispered.

Please let it be Jane Whorwood's hidden treasure.

"Jane, come and give me a hand. I need you to work at the other edge," he said.

She dropped beside him, and taking her hand in his, George placed Jane's fingers on a piece of smooth metal. If she had thought her heart rate had been running at a fast clip, it now kicked into a gallop.

They worked feverishly to free the chest. When her fingertips touched the edge of the bottom, Jane gasped.

As George wriggled the sides of the box, trying to free it from its burial site, she got to her feet. "You might want me to hold up the curtain again," she offered.

"Too late." He lifted the chest out of the ground and set it on the calico, then quickly rose. In a matter of seconds, George had the chest tucked under his arm and was making his way toward the back door. Jane grabbed the lamp and scrambled after him. It was a struggle to keep up.

Inside the house, he moved into cool, professional mode. "Lock the door, then go and check that the front is secure. Meet me in the parlor," he ordered.

She did as she was told, double checking both locks before joining George on the floor of the parlor next to their mattress. In the short time that she had been gone, George had closed the wooden shutters that covered the street-facing windows and relit the lamp.

For the first time since she had returned with their supper, George appeared to relax. Her own bubbling nerves informed her that she was nowhere near being in the same frame of mind.

They sat in silence staring at the rounded lid of the small iron chest. Jane guessed it to be a good fifteen inches in width by another ten inches deep. Large enough to hold a substantial amount of treasure.

Hopefully, their lives were about to change forever.

In what she prayed was a sign of things to come, it only took one hard strike of George's pickaxe for the lock on the chest to break. It clattered onto the wooden floor. Jane looked at it, then shifted her gaze to George.

"I think you should open it," he said.

"But you found it. Isn't there some code about the finder being the one to claim the hidden treasure?" she replied.

"Which is why I want you to open it. This has been your quest all along, Jane, and that of your father. I wouldn't do either of you the disservice by claiming that right."

She toyed with the ring on her finger. It had been a gift from her parents the year before the Scott family had set sail on their ill-fated voyage home to England. A voyage that now finally seemed to be coming to an end.

With George, there was the chance of a new life.

But will he still want it? Want me? If there is a priceless hoard in the chest, he may have second thoughts.

He moved the chest closer. "Go on. I want you to be the first to look inside."

She let out a slow breath, then with her hands resting on either side of the box, Jane gave him a hopeful smile. "I want you to know that if it's just full of old papers and the odd worthless coin, this search has not been in vain. It brought you into my life, and with that has come a grand adventure. Thank you, George."

"Treasure or no, nothing will change the way I feel about you, Jane. I love you."

Jane shifted her fingers to the top of the chest. She held her breath.

And opened the box.

Chapter Thirty-Six

Jane held the lid open for a brief moment, then slammed it shut. George's heart immediately sank.

Damn. All that digging was for nothing.

"Empty?" he asked.

She shook her head. "No," came the tiny reply.

"More papers? Please don't tell me it's another bloody cryptic clue," he said.

"No."

Jane lifted the lid once more and turned the chest so that it faced George. He immediately understood why she was struggling for words.

His jaw dropped open as his gaze took in the contents of the box.

Emeralds, sapphires, rubies, and more gold coins than George had ever seen in the one place glittered at him in the pale light. King Charles's long-lost secret treasure was lost no more.

Tears pricked his eyes. He had dreamt of such a fantastic moment but never thought to actually experience it. These things were called myths and legends for good reason—because they didn't exist.

And yet there it is.

"From the look on your face, I take it I don't need to pinch myself," said Jane.

It was a stupendous find. Priceless beyond even his imaginings, which, for George Hawkins, was saying something.

"No, but I think you should give my cheek a twist. My brain keeps telling me that I am seeing this, but it just won't sink in," he replied.

George blinked as Jane reached into the chest and retrieved a sapphire-studded ring. After slipping it onto her finger, where it fitted perfectly, she held it up to his gaze.

"I've half a mind to stroll up the front steps of the British Museum and wave this little beauty in the faces of those who didn't believe me when I told them the story of Jane Whorwood. What do you think?"

George stirred from his treasure-induced trance. "I don't think that would be wise. In fact, until our ownership of this magnificent treasure trove is set legally in stone, we should keep it a secret."

"What about Harry and Alice?" she replied.

"Even them. If word gets out, every fortune hunter in England will be banging on our door. I know the Prince Regent will want to stake a claim on behalf of the royal family. Hopefully the legal opinions Harry got are sound. The only other person who should know about this is my father. He will be able to help put our claim together and submit it to the courts."

Jane dropped the ring into the chest and sat back.

Guilt jabbed at him; his words had brought her moment of gaiety to a swift end. George closed the lid of the box and set it to one side. He shifted closer to Jane and wrapped an arm around her shoulder. "I promise that soon there will be a time for us to dance merrily, but now we have to sit patiently, wrapped in a dark cloak of abundant caution."

She frowned. "What exactly does that mean?"

It was an old saying that the members of the rogues of the road had adopted long ago. One which had served them well. And saved lives. "During the war against Napoleon, my friends and I undertook covert operations on behalf of the British crown. What we did was, of course, inherently dangerous, but you can manage risk somewhat if you stop yourself from getting a rush of blood to the head," he explained.

"I see. What you mean then is that if we take things quietly and slowly, we might get to keep the treasure. So then, what does this cloak of yours look like in our case?" replied Jane.

George placed a tender kiss on Jane's brow. He had an idea; he just wasn't sure how much she was going to like it.

"We need to do a full inventory of the jewels and coins, then we need to bury the box again."

Chapter Thirty-Seven

The area around Gracechurch Street was little better than the slums that sat close to Coal Yard Lane. After paying the driver of the hack, George jumped down from the carriage, then helped Jane to alight.

She stared up at the dull and surprisingly dirty exterior of number eighty-two. It was in sharp contrast to the rather newish-looking sign that hung over the door and shone in the early morning light.

The RR Coaching Company.

"The rogues of the road," she muttered.

As far as she was concerned, they may as well have called themselves *The Thieving Criminals Company* and been done with it.

"Let's go around to the stables. I want to know if anyone is here this morning before we get started," said George.

With the chest wrapped up in a blanket, hidden inside a bag, George hoisted it over his shoulder. Huffing with the effort of carrying the heavy weight, he led Jane down a narrow path which ran between number eighty-two and number eighty-four.

"This reminds me of the markets in Constantinople. Lots of narrow laneways," she observed.

But far less clean and without the delicious aroma of freshly baked Baklava or spices.

She pushed the thought away. It didn't remind her of the great Ottoman city at all. It was just another filthy part of the dirty cesspit that was London.

"Have you ever thought to travel back to the east?" he asked.

"No," replied Jane. That life was over; she was quietly praying that George would be the basis of her new one.

Reaching the end of the walkway, they stepped out into a surprisingly spacious mews. There was even a coach standing in the yard.

George nodded toward it. "That's the new one we bought with money that Alice brought to her marriage. The other one will be somewhere. Gus and Stephen are more than likely using it."

A middle-aged, grey-haired man wandered out from the stables and gave George a chin tip in greeting.

"Anyone else about, Bob?" asked George.

Bob gave Jane a once-over glance then, obviously deciding she wasn't going to cause any trouble, sniffed and replied, "No. The other coach might be back later today."

George pointed toward Jane. "This is Miss Scott. She is with me. We are going to examine the state of the floor in the stables."

At the sight of the large bag slung over George's shoulder, a sly grin crept across Bob's face. "My normal fee applies, of course."

George sighed and nodded. "Yes, of course. And will you be wishing to use your regular account at Coutts?"

Coutts — as in the bank to the rich and powerful? How can a stable hand afford to have an account with them?

Bob frowned. "Actually, I was thinking I might diversify my investments. Some shares in the Bank of England could be nice. What do you think?"

"Let me talk to the Duke of Monsale when he is back in town. You know he likes to make sure your pension fund is in good order. The bank does sound a sensible idea. I shall let you know what he advises," replied George.

Bob gave a nod and went into a nearby shed. He returned a moment later brandishing a rifle, which he cocked. To Jane's surprise, George didn't seem to find this behavior the least bit odd and he continued on. Bob, meanwhile, made himself comfortable in a chair which faced the rear laneway, the loaded weapon rested across his lap. From out of the shed, a dog wandered over and took up a spot next to the chair.

Jane peered at the dog. It appeared to be missing a leg. She hurried after George as he headed into the stables.

"Who is that?" she asked.

"The man or the dog?" replied George.

"Both."

"Bob and Snick. Bob gets a cut of all our jobs, while I am led to believe Snick receives a steady supply of sausages and good meat."

Inside the stables, George made his way over to the last stall. He brushed away the clean straw on the floor in the far left-hand corner, and to Jane's surprise she caught sight of a wooden door.

"Stand well back. It's heavy, and when I open the door, it will drop onto the bricks." He placed both hands on the door's large iron handle and lifted. The strain of the weight was obvious in the set of his shoulders. The door fell open with a large bang.

Jane peered into the hole as George disappeared down a narrow set of steps. His voice drifted up from the bottom. "Come on."

"Now I know what you meant when you said we were going to bury the treasure again," she called to him.

She made her way down the steps and found herself in an underground room. Against one wall was a huge iron door, bolted and locked. It had a look of secure impenetrability. "You don't take chances," she observed.

"We can't afford to," he replied.

George set his bag on the floor. After rummaging in his coat pocket, he produced a key. But to Jane's growing interest, he didn't attempt to use it on the giant padlock. Instead, he slipped it into a small, almost invisible, keyhole to one side of the lock. A click echoed in the tiny space. The main lock was a false one, designed to confuse any potential thief.

The large iron door swung open with ease.

Inside the safe were four large boxes. Each was marked with a set of initials: G.H., A.J., A.M., and S.M.

"I thought there were five of you," she said.

"There are, but once Harry got married and gave up the life, he no longer needed his." George pulled the box marked G.H. out and set it on the floor. After producing yet another key, he unlocked the box.

Inside were papers, coins, the odd gemstone, and a large wad of bank notes. It was a small fortune—enough for George to have funded Coal Yard Lane by himself.

"Why did you have to borrow money from Harry to buy the house if you have this?" she asked.

"Because there would be no point in me having all my money tied up in a house when I need it for my flee box," he replied.

"What is a flee box?"

He shook his head. "Flee box, as in, this is what I will need if I ever have to flee England. We all add to our boxes whenever we get money from a job."

"There are these things called banks, you, know? They are

likely safer than keeping your wealth under the floor of a stable," she replied.

George opened his bag and lifted the chest out. After a quick check, he placed it into the box. "I don't trust bankers. They are all thieves."

That's the pot calling the kettle black.

The box, along with the treasure hoard, now went back into the safe, and the iron door was closed and locked.

George let out a sigh of relief. "I feel so much better now that has been done. I barely slept a wink last night worrying about it."

Back upstairs and with the door and straw all set to rights, George led Jane out into the mews.

As they approached, Bob rose from his chair. At George's signal, he disengaged the rifle. "Good morning, Mister Hawkins, Miss Scott. I trust everything is all in order?"

"Yes, it is. Thank you, Bob. Your banker will receive payment instructions in good time," replied George.

"As always."

In Gracechurch Street, George reached into his pocket and produced a handful of coins. "Here, have these and get a hack to take you home. I will join you shortly."

"Why aren't I coming with you? I thought we were going to see your father and get our claim underway," replied Jane.

He shifted uneasily on his feet and wouldn't meet her gaze. "We shall see my father this afternoon. He will be in court this morning. In the meantime, I have to go somewhere. It's RR Company business. I shan't be too long." George stepped onto the road and waved his hand at a passing hack. The carriage had barely stopped before he had the door open and was bundling Jane inside.

As the hack pulled into the bustling traffic, Jane spun in her seat and pressed her face to the glass. She caught a glimpse of George as he walked in the front door of the RR Coaching Company offices.

A horrible sinking feeling gripped her. She had just stood and watched while a self-confessed liar and master thief had locked her treasure chest in his secure vault, after which she had allowed him to send her away.

"Oh, Jane. You silly girl. What have you done?"

Chapter Thirty-Eight

With no other option, Jane made her way back to Coal Yard Lane and home. As she turned the key in the front door, she paused. Would this house ever be a real home? Or was it just another stop, on her life's journey? Perhaps this afternoon's audience with George's father would give her the answer she sought.

And perhaps it might have all been a ruse, and he has just walked away with a fortune.

No. She couldn't think like that; she had to trust him. George had paced the floor until the early hours of the morning, but in the hour before the dawn, he had finally come to lay beside her on the mattress. He had held her and whispered his love.

Normally, she would have gone to visit the bakery on Brownlow Street, but her stomach was unsettled this morning and she didn't bother with breakfast. One part of Jane's mind was doing its best to convince her that the nausea was simply nerves and worry, while the other offered up a more life-changing answer. At this moment, she wasn't certain which would be the more welcome.

Inside the house, she tidied up the parlor and the kitchen,

then uncharacteristically found herself overcome with fatigue and in need of a rest.

I haven't eaten. That is the only reason.

Seated at the table, Jane pondered what she would do if indeed her feeling out of sorts was more than just that. What would she say to George?

The list of items from the treasure chest lay in front of her.

Eight large rubies
Fourteen medium-sized emeralds
Eleven large and six small sapphires
Seven gold chains of various lengths
Eighty-six gold coins, thirty-four of silver
Assorted other small gems

"And a partridge in a pear tree," she whispered.

It was an impressive haul, all of which was now securely buried in the secret vault under the stables in Gracechurch Street, along with the rest of George's escape money.

She was about to fold the list in half, when she stopped. Jane examined it once more.

The sapphire-studded ring was not on the inventory list.

"He could have made a mistake."

Who on earth are you trying to fool? He's taken the ring to sell and will keep the money.

"The only person who has made a mistake is you, Jane Scott. Why? Because you are a silly girl. Yet again you have let your heart rule your head. But this time, you might not be the only one who has to pay the price."

She put a hand over her face, desperate to keep the tears from starting.

"Jane?"

In her distressed state, she hadn't heard George open the door and walk into the kitchen.

Strong hands lifted Jane from the chair and held her tight. She wrapped her arms around his waist, not holding him, but punching George firmly in the back.

"You left the ring off the list and then you took it. How could you? I trusted you."

"If you would stop hitting me for a minute, I will tell you why," he replied.

She pulled away, out of his arms, bumping her leg on the chair. Whatever lies he was going to tell her, she didn't care. She just wanted it over.

"I took the ring. But not for the reason I suspect you think I did."

George put his hand in his coat pocket and withdrew a small box. He held it out to her. "It's in here; where the jeweler put it after he had cleaned up the stones and repaired one of the broken claws."

Her gaze darted to the box, then back to his face. "I thought . . ."

"You thought I was going to find a buyer for it and keep the proceeds for myself. Or even sell it and pay Harry back the money I owe him. Wrong on both counts. *I thought* you trusted me. Am I mistaken?"

※

George was finding that the way out from under a life of crime and lies was harder than he had expected it would be, and more painful. He now had a clearer understanding of what the boy who cried wolf must have felt like in the ancient fable. But this wasn't the time for him to nurse his injured pride. "Jane, I am not here to tell you any lies. That is in the past. I promised to be truthful to you, and I intend to keep that vow until the day I die."

"I'm sorry. I shouldn't have doubted you, but I did," she replied.

George stepped closer, brushing a hand over her cheek and catching one of her tears with his thumb. He could understand Jane's reluctance to trust him, but if they were to have a future, it was something they would have to work on. "This was my fault. I'm not used to being impetuous, and I didn't think it through."

She nodded. "Thinking things through is not something that normally goes with sudden impulses. So why did you keep the ring?"

In the wee hours of the morning, an idea had come to George, and it wouldn't let him rest. For the first time in his life, he was going to put someone else ahead of his own selfish needs.

George was relieved when Jane didn't pull away as he leaned in and kissed her.

Thank God.

"Jane, my love, you have already thought to offer me your heart, and that is beyond wonderful. What I am now demanding is your complete trust."

She raised an eyebrow. "Demanding?"

"Yes, because if there is one thing which you have taught me, it's that there cannot be love without trust. Do you love me?"

"Of course, I love you."

George took hold of Jane's hand, then went down on bended knee. His aching and tired limbs protested, but he ignored them. "Then you must trust me when I say that I love you, Jane Scott. You are my future—my whole life. I didn't want the ring on the inventory list because it should belong to you, no matter what."

Jane gently smiled at him. "My love, you should know me well enough by now to know that all I ever want is what is yours to freely give. And that is your heart."

He was more than willing to give Jane his love. She could have his entire future. "Will you do me the greatest honor and become my wife?"

She bent and kissed his lips with such tenderness that George thought his heart might burst.

"Yes, I will marry you."

And with that simple reply, he opened the box and slipped the sapphire ring on Jane's finger.

She held her hand out for a moment and inspected the ring. "It is rather gorgeous. But we should put it on the list of our claim. That way I will always know that it is truly mine."

George got to his feet and took his fiancée into his arms. "Agreed. We begin our married life on an honest footing. Start as we mean to go on," he said.

"Just promise me that when this is all said and done, you will take me to the British Museum so we can share a private moment of victory over those who mocked me when I told them that Jane Whorwood's treasure was real."

George chuckled. "I couldn't think of anything better than sticking it to each and every one of those naysayers. What unimaginative fool doesn't believe in the tale of a king's secret mistress, love letters written in a hidden code, and a chest of jewels buried in the garden of a rundown London house?"

Epilogue

It was a wonderful celebration. George even managed to smile whenever one of the many judges gathered in his family's ballroom for the wedding breakfast offered him their congratulations.

Jane found it both amusing and a huge relief. Her new husband was no longer living under the threat of the hangman's noose. His life of villainy was over and a new one as an honest man had begun.

The legal case to establish ownership of the treasure had been a surprisingly short one. Despite the Prince of Wales making known his great displeasure at the ruling, there were well-established legal precedents when it came to the subject of finders keepers.

The sapphire ring that glittered on Jane's finger was now matched with a gold wedding band. The antique jewel was worth a pretty penny, but to Jane the simple symbol of her status as George's wife was more priceless.

As the Duke of Monsale and George made their way over to where she stood, Jane considered her new husband. Monsale might well be the one with the title and a disgusting amount of riches, but George's stride now held such power that even his friend couldn't compete.

And I wouldn't swap you for all the dukedoms and money in the world.

When they reached her side, Monsale was chuckling. "I was just telling George how much of a dolt he was in not attempting to steal Baldwin's crown. That thing would have been worth a fortune."

Jane gifted Monsale with her brightest smile. "Well, of course, he didn't. My husband is, I mean, *was* a master thief; I've no doubt he spotted that it was a fake the minute he set eyes on it."

George's face turned a whiter shade of pale. His Adam's apple bobbed up and down as he swallowed what Jane could only surmise to be a large lump of surprise.

"Bah. Fancy putting one over on the British public like that. How rude," sniffed Monsale, and turned on his heel.

As the duke walked away, Jane gave a moment's pause before meeting George's gaze. She raised an eyebrow in response to the obvious look of shock, which was written all over his face. She leaned in and brushed a brief kiss on his lips. "You didn't really think that the Sultan of the Ottoman empire was going to risk sending a precious and irreplaceable treasure all the way to England, did you? He entrusted me to keep the deception a secret from everyone, including the ambassador."

"You hoodwinked the good people of London . . . What a clever woman. But the jewels were real, were they not?" he replied.

"Yes, they were real, but of such poor quality they wouldn't likely fetch much on the open market. The crown itself was made of a base metal coated in gold."

George put his arm around his wife's waist and pulled her to him. "I always wondered why you wouldn't let anyone get too close to the crown and why the room was so poorly lit.

But if the crown was a fake, why did you shoot me when I tried to steal it?"

She held his gaze. Her heart skipped a tiny beat as she beheld the love that shone in George's eyes. *He loves me, and I love him—that is all that matters now.*

"Because you had already taken something of great value from me, and at the time, I didn't think you were going to keep it safe. I decided that you didn't deserve the chance to steal anything else. Can you imagine how hard it would have been for me to gain another position if you had succeeded in snatching the crown?" she replied.

He had the good grace to look sheepish. "I was a disgraceful villain intent on stealing the crown. But I did know you had fallen in love with me and, being a heartless brute, I used it against you. As much as it hurt like the devil, I can't ever blame you for pulling that trigger." His hand drifted to the slight bump of Jane's belly and he smiled. "You were always one step ahead of me, weren't you?"

I was always hoping that you would catch me.

She placed her hand over his and nodded. "And now we walk together into this new life. As a family."

"My days of wickedness are now behind me. But I must say you had the gift of a master pickpocket when your light fingers lifted my heart and made it your own."

Jane smiled. "Tit for tat."

She'd had no choice but to take his, because hers had already been stolen by the rogue.

Bonus Epilogue

Sir Stephen Moore downed his brandy and set the glass onto a nearby table. Weddings always left a bitter taste in his mouth.

I bloody well hate these things. All that love and family stuff makes my stomach churn.

Men with titles needed heirs, and that meant marriage. Even Monsale would eventually have to succumb to it. But a man such as himself could decide his own fate. Marriage would never be on the cards for him.

And now George of all people had taken on a wife. What was the world coming to?

Though it was rather handy that she came with a king's lost treasure. And they do seem a perfect match.

He scanned the room, suddenly in need of another stiff drink.

One by one, it seemed that the rogues of the road were falling foul of that winged god, Cupid.

But Stephen was determined to remain immune. He would never marry, never have children. Of that he was steadfast and unwavering.

At that very moment, in an elegant town house not too far

away, Lady Bridget Dyson, the widow Sir Stephen had recently spent the night with, was experiencing yet another morning of feeling off color.

Cupid was sharpening his arrow.

Turn the page to read the first chapter of
When a Rogue Falls

Join my VIP readers and claim your FREE BOOK
A Wild English Rose

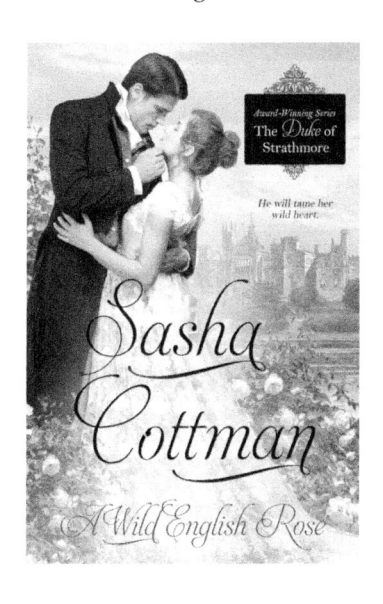

When a Rogue Falls

Earl Connor's Estate
Just outside of London

The moment Sir Stephen Moore stepped into the hallway, he sensed trouble. He grimaced at the scene which lay before him, then turned to his client. "I thought you said you had winged him?"

Earl Connor glanced in the direction of the large pool of red gore and gave a derisive sniff. "Well, he was moving a little slower than I had expected. Perhaps I got a decent shot in."

A decent shot? That amount of blood on the floor means a badly wounded man.

Stephen gritted his teeth. He hated the sight of blood, could barely stomach it.

Another night and another jealous husband. Cleaning up the private indiscretions of the *ton* was becoming tiresome. If the job didn't pay as handsomely as it did, he would walk away with no regrets.

The crimson smear on the elegant parquetry floor trailed all the way to an open door at the end of the hall. Countess

Connor's not-so-secret lover had somehow managed to drag himself away and was more likely dying in a pool of his own lifeblood in the rear courtyard.

Just what I need.

The earl took a step forward, but the bulk of Stephen's six-and-a-half-foot frame blocked his way. He placed a firm hand on Lord Connor's shoulder and levelled him with his piercing blue eyes. "My lord, I would suggest that you let me handle this. Go back to bed and pretend that nothing happened. Or better still—attend your wife. I expect she might be in somewhat of a state of distress at having her evening so violently interrupted."

"But what if the blackguard is badly injured?"

You should have thought about that before you fired a bloody pistol at the man. Not to mention you don't seem to give a damn about Lady Connor.

Stephen took a deep breath to calm his temper. Cool heads were what these sorts of situations required. "I am a professional. Handling this mess is what you pay me to do. If your wife's friend does die, rest assured it will be somewhere far from here and your involvement will never be known. Now please, hand me the gun."

Lord Connor grumbled something foul under his breath but did as he was told. The moment the earl disappeared upstairs; Stephen headed for the door.

Outside lay a young man. Blood soaked his white linen shirt, and his breathing was labored. The fact that he happened to be the Marquess of Witham only added to Stephen's already complicated night.

"Ruddy hell," muttered Stephen. He raced down the steps and came to kneel at the stricken man's side.

"The beggar shot me," groaned Lord Witham.

"Well, you were tupping his wife, so you are not exactly in a position to complain. But fear not. I have a carriage waiting outside in the street. After I get you away from here, I shall arrange for one of London's best and most discreet physicians to attend to you."

The marquess lifted his hand. "Thank you. My papa has always said you were a decent chap."

Stephen gave a brief nod in response, grateful that for once it didn't come with the usually added words of 'unlike your father.'

All of London's elite society knew Sir Robert Moore was a devious scoundrel. Fortunately, few members of the *haute ton* were aware that his son was up to his own eyes in smuggling, kidnapping, and pretty much anything else that was lucrative and illegal.

The apple didn't fall far from the tree in the Moore family.

"Now this is going to hurt like the devil. So, on the count of three, suck in a deep breath and I will lift you to your feet. One. Two—." Stephen didn't bother with three, as he hauled the stricken aristocrat upright.

"Oh! What happened to three?" groaned Lord Witham.

"I find it is always better to let the agony flow through you," lied Stephen.

Bullet wounds do tend to sting. And hopefully, you will remember how much and do your best to avoid these sorts of situations in the future. Though I seriously doubt it.

The marquess swayed unsteadily on his feet, and for a moment Stephen feared the young lord might swoon. He tightened his hold on him. "Lord Witham, I will get you out of here, but I require a number of things from you in return."

The marquess gripped the front of Stephen's jacket and whimpered. "Anything; name it. Just get me to a doctor."

"One, keep quiet. And two, don't die on me."

§

It was well after dawn by the time Stephen made it back to the offices of the RR Coaching Company in Gracechurch

Street. He arrived via the rear lane way, pulling his mount up near the stables.

After dismounting his horse, he handed the reins over to the company's one and only employee, Bob.

The craggy, old stable hand took one look at the blood stains on the front of Stephen's shirt and screwed up his nose. "Rough night, Sir Stephen?" he inquired.

Stephen rolled his eyes. "Bloody nobles—can't keep their tools in their trousers."

Bob had worked for the rogues of the road long enough not to ask for further details. He pointed in the direction of the main building. "His grace, the Duke of Monsale, and some other members of the company are upstairs in the office. I was instructed to ask you to join them once you arrived. Oh, and Lady Alice is also here."

Stephen glanced at his disheveled clothing. The fabric had dried but the metallic odor of the marquess's blood remained.

The sooner I am out of these clothes the better.

While bloodstained clothes weren't anything his friends hadn't seen before, Harry's wife was a different story. He was not going to greet Alice in this state.

His long legs took the stairs leading to the company offices three at a time. On the landing, he reached for the door handle then paused. He put an ear to the door. There was not a peep to be heard from within the room on the other side.

"Why is Alice here at this hour?" he whispered.

Because something is wrong.

His nerves suddenly tingled with premonition. It was rare for the RR Coaching Company directors to meet this early in the morning. Monsale, for one, never rose before the hour of ten. Not unless there was a crisis.

And they are all here, including Alice.

Taking a deep breath, Stephen took a firm hold of the handle and pushed open the door. The vision which met his gaze set his pulse racing.

Lord Harry Steele, Lady Alice Steele, The Honorable George Hawkins, and the Duke of Monsale were assembled around the weather-beaten, grand table, which took up much of the main room. Heads turned in his direction as he stepped through the door.

True to form, his fellow rogues of the road furnished him with their customary stony faces, but when he looked at Alice, a shiver of dread slid down his back.

Her eyes were teary, and her face flushed. The tremulous smile she offered to him, a portent of doom.

Definitely bad news. Bloody hell.

Stephen gave a quick bow. "Lady Alice. Please excuse my state. I wasn't expecting to find anyone here at this hour. Give me a minute to change, and I will be with you all shortly." He took a step toward the hallway and his room.

Monsale nodded. "Of course, take your time, my friend."

Stephen stopped dead in his tracks.

What the devil? Monsale never speaks to me like that, never uses that tone.

He spun on his heel and faced the gathering.

All the company members were present this morning. All except Augustus Trajan Jones. Gus had sailed to France two days earlier, and if all had gone to plan, he should be on his way back to England onboard his yacht the *Night Wind*, a cargo of contraband brandy safely hidden below the weather deck.

Stephen looked from Monsale to Harry and then to George. "Gus?" he managed in a voice barely above a whisper.

The mere thought of the smuggler's ship sinking somewhere in the English Channel or heaven forbid him having been captured by the customs militia filled Stephen with fear.

Gus. Sweet lord, please no.

What would he do if this was the news?

Lord Harry rose from his chair and came to Stephen's

side. He placed one hand on his shoulder, the other held out a folded and sealed letter. "I am so truly sorry, Stephen. It's your father. His lawyer delivered this to my house an hour ago. Apparently, it was the only address they had for you."

Stephen's shoulders sagged with relief. Gus was alive and well. He took the note, then without a second glance tossed it onto the table. His father could wait.

"I will make myself presentable first, then read it. A few minutes won't change the fact that the black-hearted devil is dead."

He pretended not to hear Alice's gasp of surprise. Of course, she was shocked by his reaction to the news of his father's passing. Alice Steele came from a real family—one where the members actually gave a damn about one another. Stephen couldn't remember a time when his sire had ever shared an ounce of affection with him.

And that's because it never happened.

In his room, he shrugged out of his jacket and bloodied shirt, letting them drop on the floor. He would bundle them up later and get Bob to take them to the local washerwoman in nearby Pudding Lane. She knew exactly what to do with those kinds of stains. And also, how to keep her mouth shut.

From his battered travel trunk, he retrieved a fresh, clean shirt. The act of dressing occupied his mind, keeping it from tempting thoughts of regret. Stephen was a master when it came to avoiding unwelcome emotions.

With his attire now set to rights, he checked himself in the mirror. A flannel and some water from a pitcher removed the remaining traces of last night's dirty work from his face and hands. The Marquess of Witham would live and hopefully had learned a painful lesson from his near-death experience. Hopefully.

He closed the door of his room and calmly walked back along the hallway. Stepping into the main office space once more, he gave his assembled friends a wan smile.

Let's get this over and done with.

He retrieved the lawyer's letter and slipping his thumb under the wax seal, broke it open. A quick read confirmed the news. His father, Sir Robert Moore, was indeed no longer among the living.

There were a few other pertinent details regarding balances held on deposit with various financial institutions and mention of the title deeds to the family home in Witley, but other than that, there were no actual details about how his sire had died.

No surprise there.

"I'm so terribly sorry," said Alice. The heavily pregnant wife of his fellow rogue of the road came to Stephen, arms open wide, offering comfort. He reluctantly accepted her attempted hug.

It was odd to be receiving any form of consolation over the death of a man he barely knew. A man he would not grieve.

When a tearful Alice finally released him from her attentions, Stephen turned to the other men. "Did my father's solicitor say anything else?"

Monsale sighed. "Apparently, he got into a fight with someone a week ago and a knife was produced. In the ensuing brawl, your father was stabbed. He died at Moore Manor the day before yesterday."

And no one thought to send word to me because they assumed, I wouldn't bother to make the trip all the way to Surrey.

Stephen wasn't completely sure what he would have done if someone had arrived on the doorstep of the RR Coaching Company during the past week and announced that his father was at death's door.

Probably sent them away with a flea in their ear.

Alice took a hold of Stephen's hand and gave it a reassuring pat. "When was the last time you saw your father? I hope it was a moment that you are now able to treasure."

His mind was suddenly filled with the memory. It hadn't been pleasant then, and the pain of it still burned even now. "I haven't seen my father in six years. I spied him across a crowded card table at Whites club. When I raised my glass of brandy in salute to him, he didn't even bother to acknowledge me," replied Stephen.

Harry came to his wife's side. "I'm sorry, my dear, but not all families are as close as yours or even mine for that matter. Sir Robert was never one for his relatives."

For the first time since he had received the news of his father's death, a pang of longing and regret pierced the fortress wall which surrounded Stephen's heart.

Explaining his parents to other people had always been a great source of humiliation for him. His mother had abandoned him not long after birth. After she had returned to her family in Scotland, she refused pointedly to ever have anything to do with him.

His father had been little better. He had housed, fed, and paid for his son's education, but that had been the extent of things. Familial relationships were not part of the Moore family way of life.

"Alice, thank you for your kind thoughts. I really do appreciate them. It is sad that my father is dead, but even sadder to know he wouldn't give a damn if I cried over him or not." Tears pricked at Stephen's eyes, and he hurriedly blinked them back.

His gaze drifted over Alice's head and landed on Monsale. His friend gave a brief nod. If anyone in the room could understand how he was feeling right now, it was the Duke of Monsale. Only Andrew McNeal could best Stephen when it came to having a cold, detached, and dead father.

"Well, I suppose it means a trip down to Witley is in order to claim the body and arrange a decent burial," said Stephen.

His father's timing couldn't have been worse. Stephen had

plenty of other pressing matters to deal with in London. Important things.

"Would you like us to come? I expect having some friends standing alongside you at the graveside would be nice," offered George.

Stephen considered George's kind proposal for the briefest of moments, then shook his head. "Thank you, but I wouldn't want to waste your time. The grave service will be short and without fanfare. Considering how Sir Robert lived his life, I don't anticipate having to deal with a crowd of weeping mourners."

As soon as the funeral arrangements could be made, he would bury his sire, check with the steward of his father's estate to ensure that everything was in order, then make his way back to London. There was no point in him lingering at the house.

In time, he would sell the place and leave with no regrets. It had long ago lost any promise of ever feeling like home to him.

As Harry put his arm around his wife, and they moved away, Stephen caught the baffled look on Alice's face. Of course, she couldn't understand how he felt. His lack of grief was so foreign to her view of the world. A person had to have held something and known it was theirs in order to experience the pain of loss. For Stephen, that hadn't ever been the case.

How can you mourn for something you've never had?

READ When a Rogue Falls

ROGUES OF THE ROAD
WHEN A ROGUE FALLS
Sasha Cottman
USA TODAY BESTSELLING AUTHOR

Author's Note

The cypher letters between Jane Whorwood and Charles I were real. Over a number of years, Jane smuggled gold and jewels to help restore the king to the throne, and even attempted to help him escape Carisbrooke Castle.

Unfortunately, her efforts were in vain and Charles I was executed in 1649. His son Charles II was proclaimed king in 1660. Charles II had no legitimate heirs and the crown passed to his brother.

But history has a way of coming full circle.

Diana, Princess of Wales was a descendant of two of Charles II's illegitimate sons. When her son, Prince William, eventually becomes king, Charles II will finally have someone from his bloodline on the British throne.

Also by Sasha Cottman

SERIES

The Kembal Family
The Duke of Strathmore
The Noble Lords
Rogues of the Road
London Lords

The Kembal Family

Tempted by the English Marquis
The Vagabond Viscount
The Duke of Spice

The Duke of Strathmore

Letter from a Rake
An Unsuitable Match
The Duke's Daughter
A Scottish Duke for Christmas
My Gentleman Spy
Lord of Mischief
The Ice Queen
Two of a Kind
A Lady's Heart Deceived
All is Fair in Love

Duke of Strathmore Novellas

Mistletoe and Kisses
Christmas with the Duke
A Wild English Rose

The Noble Lords

Love Lessons for the Viscount
A Lord with Wicked Intentions
A Scandalous Rogue for Lady Eliza
Unexpected Duke
The Noble Lords Boxed Set

Rogues of the Road

Rogue for Hire
Stolen by the Rogue
When a Rogue Falls
The Rogue and the Jewel
King of Rogues
The Rogues of the Road Boxed Set

London Lords

Devoted to the Spanish Duke
Promised to the Swedish Prince
Seduced by the Italian Count
Wedded to the Welsh Baron
Bound to the Belgian Count

USA Today bestselling author Sasha Cottman's novels are set around the Regency period in England, Scotland, and Europe. Her books are centred on the themes of love, honor, and family.

www.sashacottman.com

Facebook
Instagram
TikTok
Join my VIP readers and claim your FREE BOOK
A Wild English Rose

Writing as Jessica Gregory

Jessica Gregory
SASSY STEAMY ROMANCE

Jessica Gregory writes sassy steamy rom coms. She loves strong heroines and making her heroes grovel.

Royal Resorts

Room for Improvement

A Suite Temptation

The Last Resort

Sign up for Planet Billionaire and receive your FREE BOOK.

An Italian Villa Escape

Printed in Great Britain
by Amazon